GW00738363

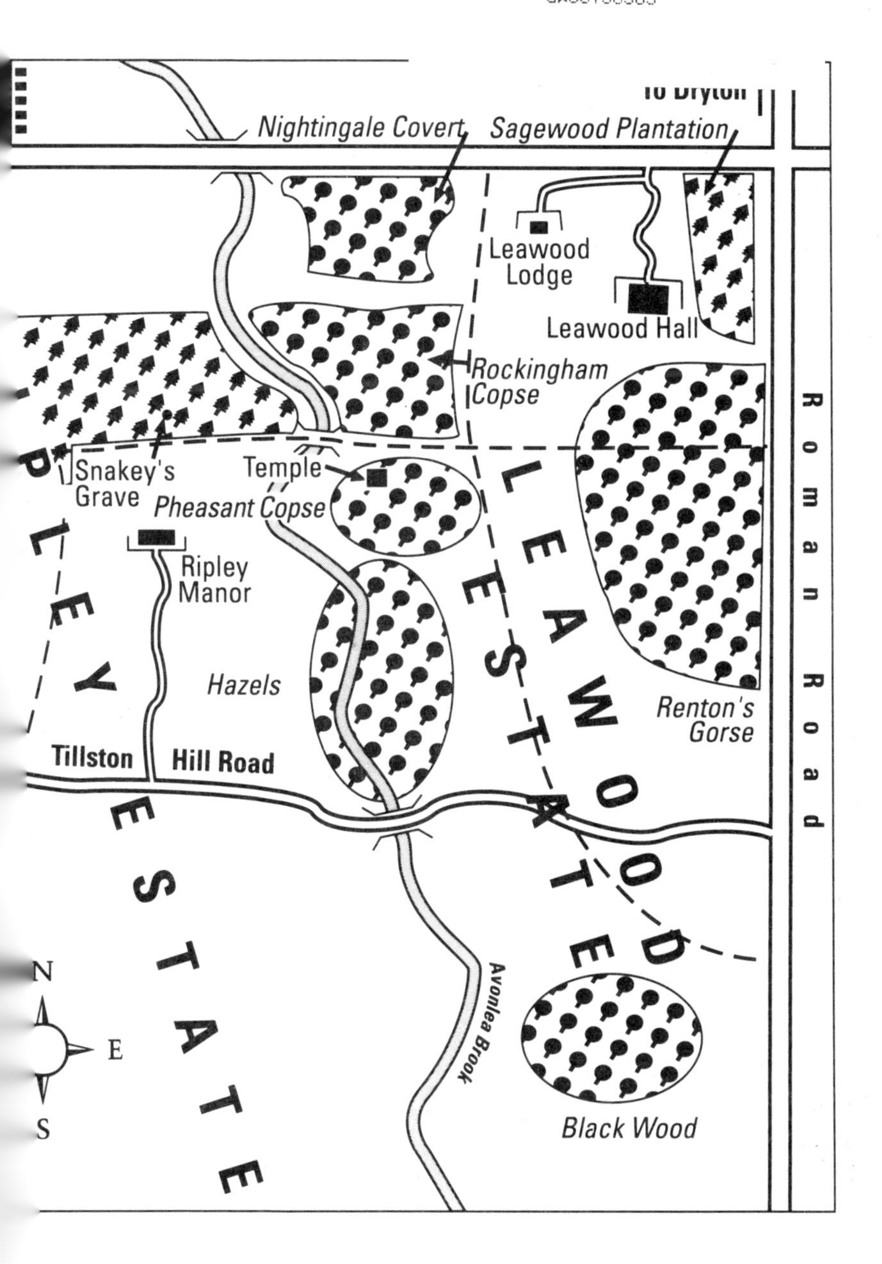
To Dryton
Nightingale Covert
Sagewood Plantation
Leawood Lodge
Leawood Hall
Rockingham Copse
Snakey's Grave
Temple
Pheasant Copse
Ripley Manor
Hazels
LEAWOOD ESTATE
Roman Road
Renton's Gorse
Tillston Hill Road
RIPLEY ESTATE
Avonlea Brook
Black Wood
N
E
S

PUFFIN AT THE CABIN

PUFFIN AT THE CABIN

J. N. P. Watson

The Book Guild Ltd
Sussex, England

This book is a work of fiction. The characters and situations in this story are imaginary. No resemblence is intended between these characters and any real persons, either living or dead.

The Book Guild Ltd.
25 High Street,
Lewes, Sussex

First published 1994

Set in Times
Typesetting by Ashford Setting and Design Services
Ashford, Middlesex
Printed in Great Britain by
Antony Rowe Ltd.
Chippenham, Wiltshire.

A catalogue record for this book is available
from the British Library

ISBN 0 86332 937 3

For Alice and Edmund French
with love from Uncle Johnnie

PROLOGUE

Those who read my account of the odyssey of the intrepid terrier bitch, Gannet, will remember that — during her extraordinary travels across the south of England — shortly after crossing the river Avon, near Downton, in Wiltshire, she was adopted by a widow called Monica Bowes-Onslow at her home, Ripley Manor. And there Gannet's puppies, two bitches and two dogs, were born. When the neighbours, to whom one of the male puppies, Puffin, was given, found that they were unable to cope with him, Mrs Bowles-Onslow took him back — though rather reluctantly, since her own three spaniels, Boadicea, Bundles and Bright, were bitches.

The adventures affecting Puffin which I have recorded in the following pages, took place a little more than a year afterwards on the Ripley land, the two private estates adjoining it and the highly developed village of Tillston which stands on the western edge of the Ripley estate, about two miles north of Downton. Those events cover a period of a little less than three weeks. That period was to be the most momentous and the most important in Puffin's life. As you will see, it was also to prove him to be very much a chip off the old block.

I

Puffin pricked his ears and sat up, his tan-and-white face inclining quizzically. He had been alerted by the sound of strange feet on the gravel outside, although the three spaniel bitches stayed curled up in their baskets on the kitchen floor, immobile and undisturbed.

Puffin knew this wasn't the vet, the postman or any other regular delivery man. Besides, there'd been no humming motor, no crunch of wheels on the gravel. Nor was it the agent, nor the housekeeper, Mrs Harris. The Jack Russell knew exactly how each of their feet touched the ground. No — this was definitely a stranger, an interesting stranger. Puffin identified the footsteps as not unlike those of the gardener, yet they were heavier, as of a man carrying a burden, or rather two burdens, one in his hand and one on his mind. He could read footsteps as well as a bird can understand the twittering messages of its mate, better than any composer reads the moods written into music, better than the shrewdest psychiatrist reads the meanings behind his patients' confessions.

When the iron knocker sounded on Ripley Manor's great front door the terrier barked and the three spaniels all looked up, alert now. Puffin was much too curious, much too jealous of the Ripley territory to be content with raising an alarm. Visual and nasal, as well as aural investigation being imperative, he scampered towards the kitchen's green baize swing door, gave it a couple of sharp blows and, having got through, galloped along the back passages and past the back stairs, knocked open the next door, raced through the library via the blue drawing-room and then through the hall, to reach the front door at the same moment as Monica Bowes-Onslow, whose step was as small and light as her bird-like figure.

While she opened the heavy door tentatively, rather as a zoo keeper might open the gate of a big cat's cage, Puffin was already receiving from the visitor vibrations, in which melancholy was mingled with kindness. He cocked his head and whined, body quivering.

'Quiet Puffin!' his mistress ordered, brushing back her wispy hair and trying to pull straight the crooked hem of her old tweed skirt which was invariably her gesture when about to meet someone. Puffin stopped whining, and shot between Monica's feet, through the doorway, and began sniffing round the man's ankles, picking up the scent of a dog, a male friendly dog according to his canny interpretation.

'I'm extremely sorry to bother you,' the man said with a pleasant smile, 'but I wonder if you'd kindly lend me a spade? I'd have it back with you within the hour.'

Monica pulled the door wider. She was more surprised at what she saw than suspicious. It was not so much the man's rugged appearance, the continental-looking rucksack set high on his broad shoulders, or even the mysterious black plastic sack which he had resting on her flagstones, that aroused her curiosity. It was more the haunted look in his eyes, coupled with his age. Year by year there seemed to be more ramblers and long-distance hikers straying onto her land, but they were nearly all young people with the cheerful adventure of youth in their hearts, whereas this was a middle-aged man, grey at the temples, lined on the jowl, which was beginning to sag a little either side of his chin. He seemed like an outdoor type, but underneath his tan a pallor showed, the pallor of a not-so-robust constitution, although he had a tall, broad physique. A single glimpse of the way the stranger stood showed her that he was a man of some style and distinction, and her hand moved to tidy her hair again.

When Puffin's nose circled the plastic sack his hackles rose and his ears twitched. Whatever it was sent a little shock wave through him and he quickly withdrew — to circle the bag from the distance of a yard away. Though the odour was quite different from the one on the man's feet there seemed to the terrier to be a connection between the two. He gave a couple of urgent yaps.

'Come back Puffin, leave the poor man alone, will you!' said Monica. Then she looked up at her visitor with a good humoured frown. 'Lend you a spade? Well, I should think so. May I ask what you need it for?'

He pointed at the sack. 'My dog has just died.' As he spoke Monica noticed spasms on his chin. Puffin was squatting now, looking keenly up at the man's wistful eyes.

'Oh, I'm very sorry to hear that. Um — I see you're not local.'

He jerked a thumb. 'No, just passing by. I've come down from the public footpath.'

'Terrible thing losing a dog. Where are you thinking of burying it?'

'There's a spot four or five hundred yards away, just off the path, directly above your house in fact, a little clearing on the edge of the evergreen plantation that I thought would do nicely . . . .'

She smiled wryly but not without sympathy. 'Oh, did

you? Well. I can't see any harm in having a dog's grave there. That lane is the only public footpath running through this part of the estate . . . You'll make the grave good and deep, won't you? I mean so that animals can't dig it up. And please take very good care of the spade. My gardener'll have a fit if it's damaged.'

'I'll return it clean as a whistle within the hour.'

'All right then, come along with me.'

She led him across Ripley's lawns on which the first leaves of autumn had fallen, then behind the cedars towards the front garden to a stone hut with a slate roof, a potting shed covered with roses, whose blooms were the last few of the year. Puffin, insatiably curious, trotted close behind the man looking up at him every few yards.

'In case you meet any of my forest people.' she said, handing him the spade, 'just say you've been to the house and that Mrs Bowes-Onslow gave permission. Oh and I'd better know your name while we're about it?'

'Clifford, Jack Clifford.'

She glanced at her watch. 'Just after three. Well. I expect you'll need some refreshment, Mr Clifford, after your travels and traumas. Would you care to join me for a cup of tea when you've returned the spade?'

'Thank you very much. May I leave my rucksack in your shed for the moment?'

'Of course. And go round to the back door when you return, tea will be in the kitchen. Come along, Puffin!'

She turned away, and her thoughts being elsewhere she did not notice that her terrier followed the stranger.

Jack Clifford took a lot of trouble choosing the precise burial plot. He tested the ground under the belt of

deciduous trees, between the conifer plantation and the footpath — in several places before instinctively finding the spot he wanted. This was just midway between two young ash trees, a little clearing, a sylvan oasis. Snakey's poor body would rest well here, he thought. Then, just as he was about to start digging he noticed the woman's little Jack Russell out of the corner of his eye. Puffin, she'd called him. The terrier was lying some twenty yards away, straight as an arrow, in a prone position, muzzle neatly framed by forepaws, ears pricked, amber eyes fixed, unblinking on the scene.

'So you've come to see the funeral's done all right, have you Puffin?' murmured Clifford. 'All right then, be my witness.' And, watched by the terrier, he set-to with the spade. When he took the body from the plastic sack and laid it in the pit of the neat, rectangular grave he had dug, Puffin jumped forward and stared down at it, quite motionless, as though held by some supernatural power.

Nearly five minutes elapsed before Clifford shovelled the soil over the prostrate, stiffening, wildly staring dog, minutes of contemplation, of poignant reflection spent squatting and gazing at the corpse. Looking down on the lurcher's black, gold and white body, his face remained motionless, but a single tear rolled onto his cheek while memories of Snakey's companionship flashed through his mind's eye. Quite unabashed, he did not care if anyone should pass along the path. He remembered a hundred little incidents since the day two years before when, a long time after their children had gone out in the world, he and Kate had chosen Snakey without hesitation or question from a litter of six, almost as though that puppy had been labelled at birth with their name.

He recalled Kate's affection for the dog and all the little adventures since he had set out on his present wanderings. . . . Snakey's low growls of warning and alarm if man or beast approached when the two of them lay out under the stars. Snakey stealing that bone from the old sheepdog on the east side of the Rother; the driver who had to jam or his brakes to avoid him on the A23; Snakey falling down the cliffside by the railway at Amberley, his descent broken only by a jungle of brambles; and he, Clifford, risking life and limb to retrieve him. Snakey careering deliriously after rabbits in those hedgerows below Beacon Hill, and having to be called away from an irate farmer; Snakey rushing away from a wasps' nest howling, tail between his legs, west of Farley Mount; and seeing off that cur that tried to steal from his rucksack on the bank of the Test; the almost understanding look on the lurcher's face when they were turned away only yesterday evening from that bed-and-breakfast place that wouldn't have dogs. And how, to keep dry, they had snuggled together under cover of an old stone pack bridge.

And he thought of Snakey this morning, ever faithful, usually at his heels, ever dependent upon him for protection. But this morning he had failed the poor dog. He had failed Kate, too, for Snakey had been very much her dog. All these memories filled Clifford's mind to such a degree that there was no space left to curse the unknown person who was responsible for Snakey's agonising death.

Looking up he noticed Puffin again. *'You understand, don't you little fellow?.* Puffin's stumpy tail flicked hesitantly. Jack turned back to the grave, and his fury built up as he started to shovel the earth in, to hide the lurcher's tortured body forever. As he did so he muttered such strong imprecations against the perpetrator that Puffin, feeling the force of them, began to whimper. Snakey's master trod the surface level, and raked it over so carefully with leaves that there was little evidence left of the grave. He took an ash twig and stuck it in the middle as a marker for himself, for he knew he must return.

He stood staring at the ground in a reverie for a moment, then checked his watch and shook his head. He hadn't noticed the time. More than an hour had gone by and he had promised the woman he'd join her for tea. Now the sun was more than halfway down to the horizon. He glanced at Puffin. 'Well, are you coming home, boy?' And he strode off down the hill, via the potting shed, to the house with Puffin at his heels. *What a lovely house this is*, he was thinking, *brick and stone in mellow combination, the same great canopied door this side as at the front. Queen Anne, probably. And those elegant terraces. The woman seemed very friendly, must be a dream to be a guest here . . . But, no, he must dismiss fantasies of comfort from his mind. He'd promised himself the sun, moon and stars for his roof, his ceiling. But October was nearly over now. What of the winter?. . .*

'How did your dog die?' asked Monica, pouring his tea.

'Poison, I suspect, strychnine,' Clifford replied simply. He was thinking that she in her ill-fitting clothes looked no less incongruous in this spick and spacious kitchen than he did in his crumpled rambling things. Yet she was a good-looking little woman.

Hovering with the teapot she gave him a sharp glance, and repeated the words. 'Poison, strychnine — are you sure of that? It's illegal. But, if so, where do you think he picked it up?'

Clifford pulled his ordnance survey map from his anorak, and with a forefinger indicated the path northwards for three-quarters of a mile. 'It must have been about there'. He turned the map round on the table for her to see. 'Is that your land, too?'

'The adjacent owner on that side is called Harrington'.

Clifford noticed that she hesitated with a preoccupied frown as though she had something more to add, but she only said: 'Milk? sugar?' and pushed them towards him.

'Is it run as a shoot?'

'Yes, it is.'

'So it would be closely keepered.'

'I would only tell you, Mr Clifford that, if ever I went there, which I don't, my dogs would never be off their leads. That is not to say that I'm making any insinuation about my neighbour. He lets the shooting to a syndicate, which is run by his son. It so happens that the son married my daughter a couple of months ago. Anyhow — returning to your dog, how can you be sure the damage was done by poison?'

'First I heard Snakey's gasps and whines. Then I found him stretched, stiff, with terrible spasms. His spine was arched, his head stretched back, eyes staring wildly, forefeet pawing the air. There was nothing I could do for him. I was pretty sure at that moment it was strychnine. Twenty seconds later he was dead. But that's not all . . .'

'What else then?'

'To prove it, I found a piece of meat a few yards away with the stuff in. I buried it.'

'A psychopath could have put it down.'

'A gamekeeper more likely.' Clifford, indignation brimming again, shook his head slowly, lips pursed in anger.

'I really think it could have been a loonie, there was a case in the local paper recently . . .'

'I'd like to get my hands on him, whoever it was.'

Monica placed a slice of cake on a plate and put it beside him. 'I'm sure you would. But what you should really do to cheer yourself up is to forget about what happened and get yourself another dog.'

Clifford shook his head again. 'I could never be so fond

of another one as I was of Snakey. My wife and I both loved him dearly. She died two months ago. He'd been a real member of the family.'

'Oh, I am sorry, I was widowed myself not so long ago. Takes a long time to heal . . . The loss of your wife must have made Snakey's death so much worse for you . . . But, really, you only imagine you couldn't get as fond of another dog — because you're mourning the dog as well as your wife. I think you would though. My husband and I had a succession of dogs. We liked each as much as the last. And just look at my lot now!' She waved a hand in the direction of the baskets where Puffin and the three spaniels lay. 'You know, you really ought to talk to someone about your wife's death, someone with a deep experience of these things . . . someone in the church perhaps.'

Clifford gave her a cynical grimace and waved his hand dismissively. 'Oh no, I wouldn't do that.'

Monica turned to him with a sudden fresh thought. 'By the way, I hope you won't think it impertinent if I enquire what you're up to — wandering across the countryside, I mean?' She gave a little laugh as though to make light of it, and raised the teapot questioningly.

'You may well ask and I'll tell you.' said Clifford, accepting another cup, which he drained quickly. 'I was so distraught and depressed following my wife's death that, after several weeks on my own — in the house we'd shared for so long — I decided to up sticks and go on a walking tour with Snakey. I'm retired, I'm my own master. I live close to Beachy Head. I'd always wanted to walk the South Downs Way from end to end . . .'

'What do you call yourself? A hobo? A romantic busker? A supertramp?'

'Nothing so grand. A common-or-garden hiker really, trying to regain his peace of mind.'

'And you've gone rather further than you originally intended. Autumn's hardly the best time for it. Have you been sleeping rough?'

He looked at her and smiled, knowingly (thinking she would like to have added 'rather a mistake at your age'.) 'We slept out on fine nights, put up at a bed and breakfast one wet night, sheltered under an old pack bridge last night .... Well, it's beginning to get dark and it looks like another showery night ahead. I'd better be going. The tea was most welcome, thank you for that and ... for providing Snakey's graveyard.' Puffin, anticipating his departure, sat up in his basket, ears pricked, staring intently.

'Where will you go now?' asked Monica. She looked as though she was genuinely concerned for his welfare, 'I won't know till I'm on the trail. Can you recommend anything?'

'Well I'd put you up here, only ...'

'No, no' Clifford interrupted, 'I couldn't do that.' He sensed that she had no real intention of having a strange man to stay. He pushed his teacup away and got up quickly, crossing to the doorway to pick up his rucksack. 'No, I promised myself a B and B would be the nearest I'd get to any real comfort. And then only for the bath that goes with it,' he added. 'You don't happen to know of a good barn or whatever nearby, do you?'

'Well there are barns, of course, but I have a better idea — as you insist on sleeping rough. If you follow that footpath, carrying on the way you were going, then down the hill ... Immediately at the bottom of my forestry plantation the path forks. Take the left fork. After a bit less than a hundred yards you'll come to a rhododendron thicket with a track cut through it, leading to a big pond, which is hidden all round by the rhododendron. Overlooking the pond you'll find an old summer house.

My husband and I spent a lot of time there when the children were small, and they used to have nights alone there when they were older. I'm afraid it's rather gone to rack and ruin now. Having been put up by my in-laws in the 'twenties it looks a bit antediluvian, but I think it's weatherproof . . . It's known by all and sundry as 'the cabin'. I'll do a sketch map for you.'

'Oh thank you, it sounds just the thing.' While she went to the kitchen dresser for paper and pencil Clifford heaved the rucksack onto his shoulders. Puffin ran close to him whimpering.

When Monica had finished her drawing she picked up the terrier and, laughing, handed Clifford the sketch. 'What a liking Puffin's taken to you . . . Well, I'll bring you some coffee in the morning and see how you're getting on. Have you got a torch?'

'Yes, thanks.' Still rather solemn, Clifford walked out into the gathering darkness.

'You're sure you can follow my directions?' she called to his back.

'Quite sure, thank you.'

Well, I wonder, she thought, closing the door behind him and looking at Puffin, cradled in her arm. *I just wonder whether you shouldn't be offered to Mr Clifford? An interesting man, a strange man, a somewhat eccentric man, but certainly a dog lover, Puffin, certainly a dog lover . . . Besides*, she thought, *Puffin's becoming a bit of an embarrassment with the three spaniel bitches.* The man's visit had reminded her that she was a lonely person despite the intensely busy life she led in the local community. She sighed and began clearing the kitchen table. She would sleep on the possibility of relinquishing Puffin and sound Clifford out on the subject in the morning.

When she let the terrier out with her three spaniel bitches four hours later, they returned but he did not. She didn't worry about Puffin, he was a bit of a loner. Like Mr Clifford?

A lovely day dawned after a night of showers, while a steady southerly breeze lifted the yellowing leaves in their thousands from the branches of poplars, maples and limes. But the oak leaves were not yet ready to be budged, staying green-gold against the black-viridian of the conifers behind them.

Not long after first light Monica, her little figure dressed in an ancient tweed skirt, a torn husky, a brown woollen headscarf and gumboots, and carrying two thermos flasks, made her way up the hill from Ripley to turn onto the public footpath. She was accompanied by the spaniels, a bobbing black-and-white escort, like magpies round a ragged falcon. She wanted to see if there was any sign of the grave Clifford had dug for his dog. She walked with small, quick, purposeful steps. After a few yards she spotted Clifford among the trees that formed the shelter belt between the path and her conifers. He stood still with his head bowed, a rather tragic figure, she thought, with the leaves of a lime tree falling lightly around him while his grey locks fluttered on his ears.

As she approached she noticed Puffin lying in that straight-as-an-arrow prone position of his, nose between forepaws, staring at the same spot that held the man's attention. She didn't have to ask: she knew it must be the lurcher's grave. But Clifford's solemn demeanour belied him. He greeted her buoyantly with 'Hello, just look at this, when I walked up here first thing I found your Puffin where you see him now, in just that very position. D'you suppose he was there all night?'

'Without any doubt,' Monica agreed. 'He didn't return

when I let them all out last thing. Pining for a dog he never knew, isn't that amazing?' She lifted the thermos flasks with a cheerful flourish. 'Here's your breakfast, Mr Clifford, coffee and sausages. You shouldn't stay on this spot any longer, you know. Too much grief is bad for anyone.'

He laughed. 'It's alright, I'm not really in the dumps now.'

'I can see you're not, so let's go down and take a look at how you've settled in.' With the dogs scampering happily ahead, she led on at her brisk pace to the glade in the rhododendron thicket where the old cedarwood cabin — with its verandah, wood-tiled roof and broad entrance steps, and seeming more like a pavilion than a summer house — overlooked the broad expanse of a reed-edged pond. This whole open space was, as she had told him, concealed on every side by the rhododendron. Tactfully, she made way for Clifford, as the present incumbent, to enter first, waiting a few moments before following him in with Puffin and the spaniels.

She glanced quickly round the interior, which still smelled strongly of musty wood, she observed, and was even more dishevelled than when she was last there. She noted Clifford's sleeping bag spread on the worn settee, his neatly folded clothes, the half-dozen paperbacks he had lined up on the shelves alongside his washing and shaving things, and her primus stove standing next to the empty rucksack in the corner.

She registered, too, the run-down state of the cabin, the broken window-frames and panes, the warped ceiling, the unhinged door, the loose floorboards. She moved to the entrance and looked beyond the verandah posts and rails, some of which had come apart, towards the pond whose banks, once planted with ornamental shrubs, were now overgrown with weeds. The stone paving around the pond was in dire need of relaying and repointing; the lawns had risen to the height of hay; the rhododendron bushes, impertinently invasive, were encroaching on every side, and she and Clifford had been obliged to raise their arms, protectively, to negotiate the approach path.

She looked up. The clearing once received the sun all through the middle of the day; now half of it was in the shadow. The broad, bright sward she had loved so well when her children were young looked quite cramped and crowded now. No wonder the water lilies had ceased to grow; they were deprived of sunlight. Going indoors again she watched Clifford take two folding chairs from their place against the wall and set them up one each side of the table.

'I'm glad to see you've made yourself at home,' she said, watching him lay the table around which she and her husband and their children had once picnicked. Now it was adorned with Clifford's hikers' knives and forks, metal plates and mugs. To her amusement the plate he had placed in front of her bore the name *Snakey*, roughly painted in blue letters on the rim. Seeing her chuckle at that, Jack reddened and hastily changed it over with his own. 'The plates are spotless, I assure you,' he smiled back.

Monica inclined her head with a touch of mockery. 'Oh, I have no doubt of that,' she said, ladling the sausages, while he produced the end of a French loaf from a plastic wrapper and rummaged in the pockets of his rucksack for salt and mustard. Puffin watched his every movement.

'Well, what are you thinking of doing now?' she asked, 'Will you head west?'

Having found what he wanted from his rucksack he stood up and faced her, a tall and lithe but rather battered looking figure, like some chieftain, the survivor of many skirmishes. 'I don't know. I've never been in such a dilemma in my life. I neither feel like moving on nor starting for home. I seem to be like a driver who lacks the will to get out of neutral. Ridiculous isn't it?' He glanced round the building. 'This is a splendid place, I must say. I wonder if you'd let me spend a few days here doing repair jobs? I'm quite a handyman. I could tidy up the outside too . . .'

She re-appraised the man. Monica rather prided herself in her judgement of people, reckoned she could detect flaws in integrity without necessarily putting the person concerned to the test. Deciding that Mr Clifford required no character reference, she gave him a firm nod. 'Well yes, why not. As it happens I shall be with my brother-in-law and his wife in Scotland for the next couple of weeks, I'm leaving tomorrow. My brother, Richard Illingworth, will have the run of the house while I'm away. He's a vicar with a parish in Guildford. He's taking a couple of weeks off . . . If you do some repairs here and tidy up outside you're welcome to stay for that period or longer if you wish. I shall expect everything to blend with the original, mind you,' she smiled.

'Naturally, I wouldn't do otherwise.'

'The village, Tillston — well, it's more of a dormitory town now than a village — is less than a mile away as the crow flies, as you'll see on your map. There's a good hardware store there; they'll order anything you need that's not in stock. Oh, and there's a bigger stores called Allason's just outside by the main road. You can call at the house for tools, or ask Mrs Harris, my housekeeper, and, of course, I'll tell my agent what the arrangement is. I think you need something more creative to occupy you than tramping across the countryside, Mr Clifford.'

'You're right, I do.'

'Did you find the paraffin lamps?'

'Yes, I took the liberty of using them as you see.'

'I'm surprised there was any fuel.'

'I shall need to buy some more.'

'I'll give you some money.'

'Oh no, don't bother, I'll fund everything. Treat it as rent.'

'And d'you think you'll want to stay two weeks?'

Clifford nodded. 'A bit more if it's OK by you? I've also got a lot of reading to catch up on and . . . I sketch.'

Monica thumbed through his book of cartridge papers, with drawings and watercolours of farm buildings, village streets, features of the South Downs, a windmill, a dovecote and any amount of sketches of Snakey, Snakey lying, sitting, standing, galloping, Snakey with a rabbit, Snakey jumping a fence, Snakey having his dinner. 'They're excellent, they're charming, absolutely charming. And I've had another thought . . .' She was silent for a moment, cradling her mug of coffee in both hands, looking intently at Puffin sitting at her visitor's feet.

'What were you thinking?'

I was wondering if you'd like to keep Puffin — I mean permanently?'

'You can't mean it? I mustn't deprive you of Puffin.' Monica noticed a fresh radiance in the man's face. 'Puffin is really only at Ripley by mistake. His mother turned up lost on my doorstep early in June of last year, and gave birth to him and his brother and two sisters a couple of weeks later. In the most extraordinary circumstances the mother was then claimed by a nice girl living as far away as Sussex. She worked in a foxhounds' kennels and was called Rose something-or-other . . . Oh yes I remember, she'd just married a vet, her married name was Peterson. Not that that has any relevance. Anyhow, it turned out that Puffin's mother, Gannet (I called her Foxy, the girl called her Gannet), really had belonged to this girl. So she took her and I found homes for the other three. (I was going to keep one but I changed my mind). Puffin's first owners couldn't cope and asked me to have him back.

'However, it hasn't been at all satisfactory. I've got too many dogs as you've seen for yourself . . . Besides which, my spaniels are bitches. I lock them up when they come into season, of course, but all the same, it isn't fair on the terrier. And it's most inconvenient for me. I see Puffin's already your devotee. I need no more persuading you'd give a dog a good life. So there . . . he's yours if you'd like him. I think you'll find him a tremendous character . . . That's settled then. Puffin's rather a good name, don't you think? Puffins, you know, stubby perky little seabirds. Puffin, son of Gannet.'

'Excellent name. Do you know anything about his sire?'

'Well, by chance Rose Peterson saw the sire just after she lost Gannet, though she didn't arrange the mating. She said he was the perfect match for Gannet. And, judging by Puffin's litter brothers and sisters, I'm not surprised at that.'

'Yes, certainly I'll take him, thank you. If he goes missing I'll know where to find him — back at the house.'

'I have a feeling he's not going to leave your side. Walk him round the farmland, by all means, but keep to the headlands if you would; and if you roam my woods it would be appreciated if you'd stick to the rides. Here — thinking you might stay for a bit — I brought along a copy of my estate map, which takes in a good deal of my neighbours' properties too.' Monica turned it round for him and pointed out the boundaries. 'As you see I'm sandwiched between two other private estates. I'd have a care if you happen to wander off my land, my neighbours can be tricky . . . Good, well now let's just make a circuit outside and see exactly what's wanted here . . .'

'I can't go at anything very fast', said Clifford, 'I have

a heart condition. It started with scarlet fever when I was a child.'

'A weak heart?' Monica regarded him closely.

'Yes, I've had angina and I suffered a slight heart attack a few weeks ago, after . . .'

She cut him short. 'Yes yes, I know. I'm very sorry. But may I ask what on earth you think you're doing trekking and living out with that risk? You ought to be tucked up at home. What does your doctor say?'

'It's OK if I take it easy.'

'Well, you can take it easy here, can't you?'

'I can and I will.'

'You've got to. By the way, you'll remember my saying yesterday that you should talk it through, I mean the subject of your wife, your mourning.'

'I remember.'

'Well, as you're now my guest, I don't mind insisting you accept a visit from my brother Richard. As I told you, I've got him staying while I'm away.'

'All right, but I'm afraid I won't have much to say to him.'

'You see if you don't. He's good at getting people to talk. That's what you need. And now we must get our tour of inspection done. Come on.'

Ten minutes later they went back into the cabin, where Monica, with a business-like flourish, checked her watch. 'Well, I must go and pack. I shall be back on November the fourteenth. I'll be most interested to see how you've got on. But don't go at things hammer and tongs. Let Mrs Harris know what other tools you require. She can probably pick most of them up at the estate stores ...' And with an extended hand and an 'au revoir, Mr Clifford,' she whisked her thermos flasks from the table, turned on her heel and, followed by the three spaniels, left for the manor.

Clifford, brightening further at this temporary solution to his dilemma and the challenge before him, looked round the room that had become his temporary home, then sat down, drank the remains of his coffee and gestured to Puffin to jump on his knee. 'Well, little fellow,' he muttered, 'you've been angling to be Snakey's replacement, haven't you? And now you've done it. As though you hadn't known all along what would happen! What a good mistress you had, careful of your needs, very bossy but generous with it. You'll find me much the same, rather less brisk and business-like though. She is a realist, Puffin. I am a dreamer. She thinks I'm a complete crank, I can tell that. Well now, we'd better get on with the job in hand, hadn't we . . . .'

The cabin reminded him of the old cricket pavilions he'd known at school; and in a reverie, conjuring the scene of a summer's day long ago, he envisaged a team of boys in white flannels skipping down the creaky verandah steps when it was their side's turn to field; or single figures with pads on their legs, bats under their arms and lowered heads, despondently removing padded gloves as they climbed the steps, having been bowled out, caught or stumped. Outside, masters reclining in deck chairs with panamas or trilbys pulled down over their eyes against the sun; and, inside, blazered boys tucking into a sumptuous tea laid out on long white-clothed tables. This building was of much the same proportions and gave off the same musty odour. It had the same sadly deserted, damp look, the same air of forlorn, seedy, neglected grandeur, of that school cricket pavilion in winter. He took stock of the wear and tear and rot, and made a list for Mrs Harris and another for Allason's. Later in the morning he and Puffin took a walk up to the manor; and in the afternoon to Allason's, the hardware store in Tillston.

Puffin was not only immediately happy in Clifford's company but, as she'd suggested, quite relieved, too, to be away from Monica's spaniel bitches. They had mostly left him alone when running loose in the garden, but when he and they were confined in the house together they had been inclined, *force majeure,* to pick on him and bully him, jealous of the place he, as a 'new boy', had secured for himself. Having been uprooted twice since his dam, Gannet, left he had felt unsettled. Now — after less than an hour — Clifford seemed like a steadfast companion, the cabin a permanent home.

Mrs Harris called in at the cabin before dusk enquiring what Clifford needed in the way of tools. 'Mrs Bowes-Onslow also asked me to say that Mr Illingworth promises to come down and see you, Mr Clifford.'

Clifford, who was standing on a chair, busy with a roof leak, did not look down. He needed to be reminded about the name Illingworth. 'Who's he?'

'That's Mrs Bowes-Onslow's brother.'

'Oh yes, of course. Well, I'm not sure . . .'

'I think he'll be here anyway.' said Mrs Harris brightly. But sensing this was not a welcome subject, she turned to Puffin. 'He's a dear little chap, Puffin, isn't he. But I do think he needs a real friend. He was used to all our spaniels. You ought to get a partner for him.'

Clifford paused, looking down from the ceiling. 'I'll think about that, Mrs Harris.'

It was dark now and, soon after she left, attracted by the night noises, he went out onto the verandah. From beyond the rhododendrons came a cock pheasant's sudden alarm cry followed by a vixen's call, telling the dog-foxes she was ready for mating, and the quavering, plaintive note of a tawny owl. Then from close by his feet, a growl at the back of Puffin's throat. The terrier's hackles stood on end. From far out in the woodland, came a long anguished howl, much rounder, hollower and more robust than the vixen's summons, like a wolf's call, ending in a wavering whine. Puffin yapped nervously; then, with ears flattened on his neck, he withdrew into the cabin. The howl from the wood sounded so full of threat, coupled with loneliness, that Clifford shuddered a little. It was a desolate call. He thought that Mrs Harris might be right and that Puffin should have a companion. The circumstances in which that was to come about, however, were not of Clifford's choosing. And the exponent of that creepy noise in the woods was to be a source of fatal trouble to them both.

II

Clifford's first couple of days in his new abode passed happily enough. He read copiously, he sketched, he made daily excursions to Tillston, buying materials he required to repair and improve the cabin, now covered on one side with the blaring crimson-gold of virginia creeper. He worked long hours putting the building's many years of neglect to rights. He enjoyed the constant company of chirpy, affectionate Puffin who soon proved an ideal replacement for Snakey. And following his steep South Downs trek Clifford knew his unreliable heart would benefit from spending these days in relative idleness, these nights under one reasonably comfortable, if spartan, roof.

Above all here he felt at one with nature, and — particularly since Snakey's death — a new response to the wildlife around him. As a watercolourist he delighted in such little joys as the auburn and red of the maples, the ruddy crab apples now beginning to fall from their coppery branches, the delicate grey and iridescent, mauve and green of the wood pigeons descending to drink at the forlorn lily pond. Then there were the vivid splashes of lichen and moss on the stone surrounding it, and all the autumn colours set against the azure and white sky and vivid sunsets. He noted the rushing, chattering migrations of fieldfares and redwings. He relished the odours of the newly fallen leaf, of the woodsmoke curling and drifting from the forest workers' fires, and the stench of fox after one of those predators had prowled round the building in the night. And he was thankful to kind Monica Bowes-Onslow for all these things.

This was for Clifford at first a marking-time period, a philosophical phase in which to rearrange his priorities, his sense of the precedence of creation. He had given many moments to such speculation during the trek from Beachy Head. And now he concluded that the fleeting lives of men and women were mostly petty and vainglorious; that the world of creatures, indeed the world of wild Nature in general, was more beautiful and more meaningful than the superficial lifestyles and ambitions of human beings.

Friendship with Snakey, and now with Puffin, had taught him that dogs' characters were frequently more congenial than their masters' — and that included his own.

Since Snakey's death he recognised in himself a new regard for the sanctity of animals. On his second evening there during one of the long walks he gave himself with Puffin, he watched some badgers at play; and how his heart went out to them! Two days later when the local foxhounds trotted by — it was the last morning's cubhunting before the opening meet — he implored the huntsman to give the sett a wide berth. The man said he would oblige. A little later, when he came across some boys ferreting near the same place, he asked them whether they had permission. When they admitted they had not, he pretended he was the agent and sent them packing. On another occasion, when he saw a cat stalking into the rhododendron enclosure with a live great tit in its mouth and then start to play with the bird, he set Puffin on this feline felon, which promptly dropped the tit. Puffin chased the cat up a tree and, in true terrier fashion, wouldn't stop barking at it. Then Clifford was ashamed of himself for being angry with Puffin for causing the cat distress. There was more to learn of nature, he reminded himself, than he could ever know.

Everywhere around Tillston he took note of the apparently inexorable surge of development: new residential areas, old barns converted into dwellings, woodlands and hedges removed for agriculture. Beauty spots were converted — into a commercial fishing lake here, a new golf course beyond the Brinkworth estate there. There was more space for people, their food and their diversions, less for animals. And the rush and impatience everywhere, with farm animals used as automatons forced to move at human speed, horses and ponies neglectfully overwintered, exploited not loved . . .

He was aware that he had become oversentimental; and he realised, too, that his new frame of mind was partly the result of the effect on him of Snakey's cruel death. But, as he became increasingly attached to Puffin, this confusion of affections diminished. Meanwhile, that eerie sound rang out every night in the forest, a sound to which Clifford paid little attention at first, but one that fascinated Puffin. It was that same long plaintive howl, that wavering call, as of a lonely beast summoning company, a ghostly noise which Puffin — going out, ears pricked, hackles standing, onto the moonlit verandah — found at once thrilling and forbidding, alluring and terrifying. It was like a wolf's call.

A little over a mile north of Jack Cliffford's primitive, isolated and temporary abode lay the hamlet of Coneyhurst Corner, whose community is centred on a row of a dozen little semi-detached houses known as Ivy

Cottages, built in the 1920s. The end house, number 24, was occupied by the Sewell family, the owners of a lurcher called Dusty. At the time of Clifford's arrival in the vicinity Dusty was having a bad time.

This dog had, in contrast, enjoyed an almost idyllic early life. Dusty (by a greyhound out of a brave collie), having been the apple of his dam's eye, grew up strong, confident and at one with the world. The couple who bred him also regarded him as best of the litter, so he was the one they kept. The first year of his life, spent in the company of his mother and his indulgent owners, was a year of unblemished happiness. Tragically, soon after that, he was stolen while the couple were holidaying in Wales, then abandoned, then collected as a stray and eventually incarcerated in an unregistered commercial animal shelter. It was the Sewells of Coneyhurst Corner, Wiltshire, themselves also holidaying in Wales at the time, who bought him.

Having acquired a small hoard of silver and being obsessed with the notion that attempts would be made to steal it Ted Sewell decided they needed a guard dog, and, of all the canines in that animal shelter, Dusty was the one which most impressed him. Sewell went ahead with the purchase — without consulting his wife. He named the dog Dusty — with good reason, for his coat, once so glossy black, gold and white, was now lustreless and dirty. Nor did the Sewells do anything to improve Dusty's condition. They kept him at the bottom of their little garden plot, on the end of seven feet of chain, with a beer barrel for his kennel. They fed him and they removed his excrement, but they never walked him, never talked to him or played with him, never let him off that seven feet of chain. Having once experienced warm and constant affection and a life brimful of activity Dusty now felt unfit, bored and unloved. A couple of days after

Clifford first occupied Monica's pondside summerhouse, however, a melodrama broke the monotony of Dusty's life. It began with a complaint.

A combination of the dog's too-tight collar and a night spent barking had given Dusty a sore throat and a sore neck. In his yearning for communication he'd been answering a farm dog's yap and, in his excitement, while patrolling back and forth in front of his barrel kennel, he jerked painfully on the short tether of his chain. Not surprisingly, he'd kept several neighbours awake. But all of them, with one exception, were too frightened to complain to Ted Sewell, who had the reputation of being a violent and abusive man. That exception was 16-year-old Jerry Fuller, who had recently left school and was still living with his parents at number twenty, Ivy Cottages. Jerry, a great animal lover, could see Dusty from the window of his bedroom and was sorry for the dog, although he was aware that so far as the law was concerned, there was nothing wrong with the way the animal was kept. He usually slumbered happily through most things, but on that particular night, owing entirely to Dusty's 'monologue' his parents had scarcely enjoyed a wink's sleep and Jerry was determined to intervene on their behalf.

'I really wouldn't do it', his mother warned. 'That Mr Sewell could turn very nasty, Jerry, and I don't like the sound of his wife neither' (which was precisely the reaction of all the other neighbours who had been kept awake). But the boy was angry. He was as upset about the Sewells' treatment of Dusty as the fact that the lurcher, through no fault of its own, had become a public nuisance. 'They don't frighten me, Ma', he replied, 'I'm havin' it out with 'em!'

Jerry, a stocky lad with thick ash-blonde hair brushed straight back from his forehead, and with a stubborn look in his ice-blue eyes, called on the Sewells on his way to work — a building site near Tillston. Walking up the brick path of number 24, which was flanked by their overgrown little garden, he immediately noticed the weal on Dusty's neck where the collar had choked in those hours of darkness. Jerry saw too, the shallow trench the dog had created, padding round and round on the closely circumscribed area of its existence. So his heart went out with compassion to the miserable, dowdy creature that lay there. Priding himself, as he did, in having a way with dogs, he scratched Dusty behind the ear and patted him before turning to the Sewells' front door.

Looking up at the semi-detached house, he observed its dismal façade. Its dirty stuccoed wall, its peeling window-frames, broken drainpipes and neglected garden made it stand out among this row known as Ivy Cottages, as a sinister place where love was scant. He braced himself to announce his mission. He gave three firm knocks, which were answered by a figure familiar to him, a slatternly woman twice his age, whose expression was surly and impatient. 'Sorry to bother you', he said, 'I'm from number 20, it's about your dog . . .'

'Yeah? Well, Ted, my husband, he deals with Dusty and he's gone to work.'

'Maybe, but your dog keeps my ma and pa awake.'

A child, a girl of about twelve years old, had crept round Mrs Sewell's side. 'Oh, Mum', the child pleaded, 'let's get rid of Dusty, I don't like Dusty.'

'Sh-sh, Candy!' ordered Mrs Sewell flicking the girl's shoulder. She turned to Jerry again. 'Yeah, the dog has got bad, ain't he. All right young feller, don't you worry no more about Dusty, we'll keep him quiet, we'll shut him up.'

'Oh, does that mean you'll lock him up somewhere? I wouldn't want your dog to suffer, I really wouldn't.'

'Don't you mind about that, it means we'll stop his racket, see? Simple. We'll keep Dusty quiet, we'll shut him up.'

'Well . . .' Jerry started. But Sharon Sewell closed the door in his face.

That night Jerry heard the distant barking of a farm dog; and, from the direction of the Ripley woods, a long drawn-out howling like that of a wolf, but not a sound from Dusty. And it was the same the next night. Early the following morning, leaning from his window, he saw the lurcher pawing at its muzzle. Something was the matter. Curiosity getting the better of him, Jerry decided to take a closer look.

He dressed quickly and tiptoed past his parents' bedroom. If they knew he was going to examine the Sewells' dog, they'd have been horrified, he knew that. But Jerry never gave the matter a second thought. As Dusty's kennel was no more than a couple of yards beyond the Sewells' wicket gate, he spotted the trouble straight away. Three elastic bands had been stretched round the dog's muzzle, cutting into the pelt as well as locking its jaws. He bent down and gently stroked Dusty's head as he had done before. Then, one by one, he removed the rubber bands. The lurcher gave its muzzle a rapid succession of licks, fixed Jerry's eyes trustingly with its own and flicked its tail in gratitude. A moment later the cottage door burst open and Dusty's ears flattened, while it gave a low, deep growl. It was the child, Candy. 'Here, you can't do that!' she screamed. 'My pa put them bands on Dusty.'

'They were hurting him,' Jerry objected.

'Those bands don't do him no harm,' said Candy Sewell. 'They stops him hollering. We takes them off when he has his dinner, then we puts them back on.'

'Well they can stay off now surely, seeing it's daylight?'

Jerry put the offending ties in his pocket.

'It's none o' your business it ain't. I'm getting Pa.'

Jerry didn't in the least mind facing Mr Sewell. He stayed in his crouched position, stroking Dusty and waiting.

''Ere, what you think you're doing with my dog, eh?' he heard half a minute later. Sewell's bulky menacing figure stood over him, hands clenched, beer belly shaking, eyes blazing.

Jerry got up to face the man, and spoke coolly. 'I don't think it's right treating a dog like this, Mr Sewell.'

Sewell took another pace towards him, breathing heavily. 'Oh, yer don't, don't yer. And what's it got to do with you, lad, eh? That's what I want to know.'

'I like dogs, that's what. Couldn't you keep 'im loose indoors?' Jerry asked reasonably.

'That pooch ain't fit to be in anyone's house. 'Sides he's supposed to be a guard dog.'

'How can he be a guard dog when 'is mouth's tied up?'

'Sewell's temper was exhausted. He jabbed at Jerry's chest with a forefinger. 'Look here, lad, who d'you think yer talkin' to? Just you stick to what concerns you and nowt else, right? And get off of our ground or I might be tempted to do something dangerous.'

'All right. I'm leaving, Mr Sewell, and I'm going to the police about you.'

'You do that lad, and get out of here in double quick time, too, or you won't know what hit you, see?'

Despite Jerry's brave threat his heart was thumping as he walked home.

'. . . The cheek of it', Sewell was telling his wife, 'that young bloke said he was reporting us to the police, and he looked as though he meant it an' all.'

'Don't blame me, dear, I said at the start we don't need

no guard dog. It was *your* wonderful idea, not mine. You never even told me when you went to that kennels in Wales. You just returned with the rotten thing, didn't you?'

'Now then, Sharon, it's no good going back on that,' said Sewell. 'Dusty's a load of trouble and no mistake. Question is what are we going to do now, that's what matters.'

'Have it put down by the vet, that's what I'd do.'

'You're joking, dear, you are. You pays twenty quid just for going through the door of one of them places, and by the time you walks out, so the lads tell me, it's another thirty. Put it down? ... well I do agree with you, love, it needs killing. I can put it down easy and cheap, by bringing a shovel down on its head.'

'Oh Ted, *really*, that's not my idea of funny!'

'I'm not joking. I'll do it first thing in the morning. Easy as wink. Reckon I could have Dusty dead as a doornail with three good hard hits. I wouldn't have no conscience neither 'bout doing in a useless animal.'

Sharon Sewell eyed her husband silently, askance for a moment and shivered. *You would do it, too,* she thought, while an alternative plan took shape in her artful mind. 'Not in the morning, Ted, we shouldn't do anything on the spur like. You just get off to work first thing and we'll sort something out in the evenin.'

'We'll sort something out alright — when I gets in from work and no later. Dusty's a luxury we can't afford.'

'Dave picking you up first thing?' his wife enquired casually while thinking hard.

'Yeah — what you want to know for?'

'Well. I need the car, that's what. Must go shoppin' in the morning.' *(No way am I going to have a dog hammered to death here,* she was saying to herself, *I won't stand for any messy business. I don't mind paying for it out of me housekeeping.* She was by nature a dissembling woman.)

Jerry Fuller stayed awake a long time that night. He heard the yapping farm dog again and the distant wolfish howl and listened, with some relief, to Dusty's free response. This was better than being haunted through the night by the thought of the Sewells' dog still muzzled by elastic bands. He had taken a strong liking to Dusty. He was more determined than ever to be the lurcher's protector, but he still hadn't been to the police. Though he wasn't quite sure what to do about the poor creature, he was convinced the dog looked to him, Jerry, as its potential saviour. He'd be seventeen very shortly and was about to move out of Ivy cottages to a place of his own. Then he could become Dusty's owner.

Far into the night he imagined the Sewells coming to him, saying they couldn't manage the dog.

He would have Dusty's company on the building site during the week and romp with him for mile upon mile at the weekends. Once he fell asleep the barking did not disturb him at all. But the Sewells had made him no such offer.

Mrs Sewell phoned the Tillston vet next morning within minutes of her husband leaving the house. 'Got to have our pet dog put down, it's urgent. Can you fit it in today, early as possible?'

'Bring him round at eight forty-five will you then? You'll be first,' replied the assistant.

Sharon Sewell took a cool look at Dusty, deliberately blotting out the memory of how touched she had been by the dog's engaging character during the first month or so after her husband had made the purchase. She steeled herself for the grisly task in hand, and addressed the dog with a sour mutter; *we've fed yer regular, we've given you yer own little house and shelter and what do we get in return? — a load of trouble.* Biting her lip, she contemplated the lurcher for a few seconds longer before checking the time. Then she unclipped his chain, replaced it with a leash and led him to the car.

'Oh Mum, wait!' It was Candy skipping out. 'Can I come too?'

'I don't think you ought to, love, it won't be nice.'

'Oh yes, Mum, please. I could help you. 'Sides, I want to see Dusty killed. Always hated him. I'd like to see the end of him.'

'Oh, alright then. Here, take him. Put him on the back seat and hop in next to me, there's a good girl. And don't say a word about this to your dad, see.'

'Alright, Mum.'

Dusty was so relieved to be unshackled from the beer barrel that he wagged his tail and licked his muzzle in eager anticipation as he was bundled, albeit impatiently and roughly, onto the back seat of the car. Within five minutes they were at the veterinary surgery, in Tillston's new shopping centre. The waiting room was empty, with the exception of an old man holding a wicker basket containing a loudly mewing cat.

'Mr Tomkins would like a word with you out here, Mrs Sewell, he won't be a moment,' said the white-coated assistant. At that Sharon Sewell's heart beat a little faster while, sitting on the hard bench fixed to the wall, she held Dusty between her legs. *Would the vet refuse to do the job? Oh, if only it was all over.*

Dusty, relieved of the monotony of the beer barrel at 24, Ivy Cottages, was taking an interest in this new life around him, watching all the activity in the reception area, sniffing the floor, intrigued by the different scents of recent four-legged visitors. Curious to know more about the plaintive cry coming from the wicker basket held by the old man, he stood up and wrinkled his nose towards it. 'Siddown! Siddown will you!' hissed Sharon Sewell, bringing the end of the lead down sharply on his flank, while Candy gave him a kick on his hind quarters. Someone entered the surgery with a bulldog and sat next to the old man. Dusty who had only set eyes on one other dog in recent months, wagged his tail, cocked his ears, and whined in greeting. 'Shuddup Dusty, behave yerself, will you!'

At that moment the vet came in with a pleasant smile and asked them to follow him into a second waiting room. 'I really don't like to do this you know, Mrs Sewell. We only euthanise in exceptional circumstances. Are you certain you can't cope with him?'

'He's impossible. My husband and me's come to the end of our tether.'

Candy piped up, with a meaningful grimace towards Dusty: 'That's right, our dog's got to be killed. He's nasty.'

'Have you tried offering him to an animal shelter?' the vet wanted to know.

'Oh yes, they're all full up,' Mrs Sewell lied. 'My husband says if you don't do it he's going to do away with it himself, banging it on the head with a shovel.'

Mr Tomkins winced. 'Well in that case I suppose I'd better euthanise him. Pity — he doesn't look in the best of health, but he seems to have quality. Er — you'll not be acquiring another one in your present circumstances will you, Mrs Sewell?'

'No, not never, we've learned our lesson.'

'All right then, bring him through will you. Your little girl will be all right waiting here, won't she? There's some comics in the corner.'

'Oh no she won't. Candy wants to see it happen, and I need her help.'

'That's right', echoed Candy, 'I want to see what you do to him.'

Mother and daughter started moving towards the surgery door. But Dusty, prompted by some premonition of danger, the fear that invariably grips animals at a veterinary surgery — even animals that have never been taken to the vet before — dug his toes in. Something sinister seemed to go on behind that far door, while a certain fresh determination in the demeanour of Mrs Sewell and her daughter prompted the dog to resist. He shuddered, as though with dementia. Sharon Sewell and Candy, both gripping his collar, skidded him through the door and along the passage and, with the help of the vet's assistant, lifted him onto the operating table. Dusty was panting as well as shivering now, and his eyes were dilated with terror like someone about to be pounced upon by men with knives.

'Just hold him tight while I prepare the needle,' said Mr Tomkins, concentrating hard on the level of the sedative. Mrs Sewell held Dusty's collar, and Candy clutched a fold of skin on his back, while the nurse assisted the vet. Dusty's shivering abated. His eyes swivelled towards his back and every muscle in his body tightened. He was crouched for a spring. 'Here we are then,' said Mr Tomkins, flicking the hypodermic. But his words distracted the Sewells, who looked up for a second and slightly released their grip. In that moment of relaxation Dusty wrenched himself free and, with the lightning speed of a striking cobra, leaped to the floor. The door had not been fully closed. He squeezed past it, scurried down the passage, tail between his legs and through the waiting-room's swing door. As he scratched and whined at the front entrance to the surgery, Sharon Sewell strode towards him, followed by a hysterical Candy crying 'Here, come back here, you silly brute!'

Just then a fat woman entered with a chihuahua pressed to her bosom. Dusty shot between the woman's legs, causing her to trip and let go of the chihuahua which landed, yelping, on Candy's face. In a flash Dusty was careering down the street. His navigational sense, coupled with a passion for survival, guided him in the direction of the only place of security he remembered, the Sewells' house and the beer-barrel kennel by the garden path.

Mrs Sewell dashed out of the surgery yelling 'Hurry up, Candy!' and was in her car immediately. But, once in the driver's seat, she paused with second thoughts. It did not occur to her that the dog would instinctively head for home. Her fingers drummed the steering wheel. *Well — why not let the animal go missing? That way I'll not only avoid the trauma of the vet's needle, about which I'd felt extremely squeamish, but I'll also be saved the vet's bill. Yes, that'd be best, I'll just let Dusty vanish, tell Ted I took him for a walk and he escaped.*

Candy banged her fists up and down on her knees in a frenzy, shouting 'Come on Mum, what are you waiting for? We'll never catch him if you don't go now. I wants to see him back on that vet's table!'

Slowly and thoughtfully, Sharon Sewell turned to her daughter, speaking quietly. 'We'll let him go, Cand, easiest way out now. And what we'll tell your dad is we took him for a walk an' he escaped. Or we might say when we let him off his chain he run away. And, now we're here, we may as well do a bit of shopping, right?

'Oh, oright, Mum, But Mum . . .'

'Yes?'

'I did want to see 'ow the vet does it.' Candy lifted her fists from her knees to her eyes and sobbed. But still her mother wouldn't move. Mrs Sewell passed her tongue from side to side between her lips, drumming the steering-wheel with her finger-nails and looking reflectively through the windscreen. *How's Ted going to take all this?*

she was wondering. *How?* At last she gave a heavy sigh, got out of the car and, followed by a bitterly disappointed Candy, made for the shops.

'Mum?,' said Candy on the way.

'Well come on, what is it now?'

'I want to go to the playground.'

'You spend more time on those swings than any child in the county — *No,* Candy!'

'Oh come on, Mum, as I didn't see Dusty killed . . .'

'Oh alright, but only ten minutes, not a second more.'

'Thanks, mum, I love them swings.'

Five or six hundred yards from the surgery Dusty turned off the village street, circled the roundabout and raced into the main road. Just then, an elderly bespectacled shopper, driving away from Tillston, saw his fleeting figure a fraction too late. She slammed on her brakes, but the wing of her mini metro caught Dusty a glancing blow on the buttocks. The old lady pulled into the side, hauled herself out of the driving seat and shuffled to comfort him. He sat on his haunches by the kerb, bellowing disconsolately. The shock and pain of the blow to the lurcher quite eclipsed the terror of the vet's surgery.

A passer-by, a younger woman, who witnessed the accident, addressed the driver. 'Oh, poor thing, you struck it quite a blow, but you couldn't have missed it, you mustn't blame yourself, ran straight into you.' And when she stooped and stroked Dusty's head, Dusty licked her hand and looked up beseechingly.

That morning Clifford, having taken further stock of the cabin's wear and tear and rot, and having placed an order for some nails and lengths of wood at Allason's, proposed to pick them up from the hardware store as soon as it opened. But, with dawn breaking so radiantly and invitingly, he decided to take Puffin on a detour first. They struck off south to meet the Old Green lane, the dividing line between the Ripley and Brinkworth estates, a path thickly bordered with jungly overgrown hedges, mainly of hazel, holly and field maple. This route, heavily pockmarked with hoofprints (probably from the hunt, he reckoned) was broad enough for vehicles and had, he judged, been an important road long before the age of the combustion engine.

In this open autumn, free of frosts, blackberries and elderberries still shone out of their bronzed foliage between the taller trees, and rose hips and hawthorn berries glistened scarlet and crimson, contrasting with the silvered midnight blue of the blackthorn's sloe. The season of mellow fruitfulness might be overstaying its welcome in Mother Nature's book, but Clifford was thankful for autumn's extension, thankful to Monica for the cabin, thankful he was not at this moment trekking back with no Snakey to Beachy Head.

As they came round to the Tillston Hill road again Puffin gave chase to a rabbit. Jack's heart missed a beat as he heard a screech of skidding and brakes on the tarmac. Racing forward he climbed over the first stile, only to be confronted by a red-faced man leaning out of his car window shouting 'Why can't you keep your bloody animal under control?! . . .' Clifford merely apologised and thanked heaven that he hadn't lost a second dog in the space of a few days.

Fifty yards more down the thicket-flanked lane, flocks of fieldfares and redwings flew across his front. As he was wondering where they had spent the summer and what hazardous journey they had made to reach Wiltshire, he smelt smokefumes, and peering through a gap in the bordering trees he saw a white pall swirling high into the sky, rising from the wood across the field to his left. He unfolded Monica's estate map, which took in quite a bit of the Brinkworth territory. The copse in question was called Jenkin's Wood. The timber being dry, perhaps the fire had been started by a careless forester? With Puffin romping ahead he started across the stubbles to investigate.

Drawing nearer he noticed that the trees he had seen from the lane were only on the periphery of the wood. Judging by their height and girth they must have been at least a century and a half old. Behind them there were no trees at all. Three bulldozers were pushing the remaining roots onto a couple of enormous bonfires. Clifford inhaled the acrid-sweet odour of burning deciduous which began to sting his eyes. He came alongside a young bespectacled woman in gumboots, headscarf and an old overcoat. 'Crying shame, isn't it', she said biting her lip and sighing, but hardly turning to him. 'Just think of the wildlife that's been destroyed along with the trees.'

'Why are they doing it?' asked Jack.

'They're using that last hurricane as an excuse to get rid of the lot.'

'Looks like Britain's answer to Brazil's destruction of the rainforests,' said Clifford. 'What's its future then?'

'It's going to be planted up with conifers. We tried persuading the landowner to let it go back to nature. Half the trees were still upright. We asked him to consider letting the rest rot down. The fungus would have taken over and drawn the wood into the ground and young trees would've soon started up, as we informed him ... He told us to mind our own business. So there we are; twenty acres of ancient deciduous woodland gone for firewood and all we can see now is the roots piled up and smoking. There were nightingales here and white admirals and lesser spotted woodpeckers and wild service trees, and now none of any of them. Criminal isn't it? All making way for commercial evergreens.' She stared, expressionless, straight ahead.

'You said "we". Who's "we"?'

'I'm from the County Naturalists' Trust. The present owner's father let us have a nature trail through it and didn't mind how often we took small groups here to enjoy it. He'd turn in his grave if he saw what his son's doing to . . .'

The young woman failed to finish her sentence. As she was speaking a man, who appeared to be in charge of the clearance, jumped the perimeter ditch and shouted 'What d'you think you're doing on this field? This is Mr Edgedale's property.'

'I know that,' said the young woman calmly. 'We're watching your work with some dismay. It's sacrilege, that's what.'

'Well, go and watch it from the public footpath!' He pointed towards the Old Green lane.

'I'm not moving,' the woman told him. 'Unlike you, we're doing no damage.'

'I'll get someone you won't like onto you for trespass if you don't get out.' The man withdrew into what was left of Jenkin's wood, while the young woman stood her ground. Clifford glanced at his watch. Determined to reach Allason's store by opening time so that he'd lose not a second of daylight with his work on the cabin, he bade her good luck and good-bye and made his way to the lane, silently agreeing with all her conservationist sentiments, but putting the incident to the back of his mind for the moment. Nor was that the finish of his Brinkworth experience. As he recrossed the stubbles a man applying fertiliser stopped his tractor straight in front of him, switched off the engine and shouted 'What the bloody hell d'you think you're doing walking across this lot without permission? Get back to the footpath and take that effin' little dog with you!'

'That's just where I'm going', said Clifford without stopping. Although he very much resented the abuse, which, coupled with the reprimand received at Jenkin's wood, rankled with him some of the way to Allason's store, the last thing he wanted just now was to earn a name for trespass and so be the cause of embarrassment to Monica with her landowning neighbours. So he kept his peace.

Weighed down with sombre thought, along with his shopping, as he left Allason's he did not immediately notice the scene of Dusty's accident. It was Puffin, hearing the dog's whine, who alerted him to the drama. A little way up the roadside to their left the two women, the driver and the pedestrian who were involved, were at that moment contemplating the Sewells' injured lurcher.

Puffin witnessed the scene within seconds of the woman on foot arriving. Leading Clifford out of Allason's warehouse the terrier gave a couple of quick barks, alerting his master to the incident. Puffin raced on for a closer look, then squatted in his prone position, nose between forepaws, whining with a fascinated interest in the injured Dusty. Clifford followed, stopped, stared and blinked with amazement. The closer he drew, the more uncannily this dog resembled the lurcher he and his wife had loved so well, Snakey now buried between Monica's trees beside the public footpath above Ripley Manor. It was as though the dog had come back to life. This one not only bore the same classic lurcher conformation as Snakey but had, too, the slightly longer collie coat, not so brindled as other lurchers he had known, more distinctively colour marked black, gold and white like a collie. This one could be a litter-brother, a twin — could be Snakey resurrected from the dead. Clifford could hardly believe his eyes. 'Badly hurt is he?" he asked the women.

'Oh, hello . . . just bruised by the look of it,' replied the younger one.

'Let's see how he walks,' Clifford suggested, lifting Dusty gently by the collar. The dog was very lame and his head hung low, but he struggled along without any resistance and sat down obediently when Clifford stopped and inspected his collar. 'No identification and obviously a stray by the look of him. I'll take him home and see what I can do for him,'

Both women were pleasantly surprised at this stranger's intervention. 'Oh, that's very kind and saves me a lot of trouble,' said the motorist. 'But could you please give me your name, in case there are enquiries.'

'Clifford, Jack Clifford.'

'And perhaps I should know where you live, too.'

'No fixed address. But, anyhow, don't bother with that, I'll tell the police first thing tomorrow.'

'Oh well, that's all right then.'

'He'll be quite safe with us,' added Clifford, pointing smilingly at Puffin who was standing on his hind legs, licking Dusty's cheek. 'Come on, Puffin!' And Dusty followed without demur, very lame but just managing to walk on all four legs.

That night the long eerie howl that had regularly disturbed Clifford was repeated. As soon as it began Puffin and Dusty went out onto the verandah and, as though in a trance, stood stock still until the noise died away.

Clifford decided not to tell the police about Dusty after all. He was worried lest the dog should be returned to its owners, who were obviously not responsible people. Following a day's exercise round the Ripley estate Dusty, though still rather nervous, looked healthier and happier, and, like Puffin, was reluctant to be far from his benefactor. Even on those occasions that Clifford stopped, got out his sketch pad and pencil and squatted on a fence or against a gate, to draw, the dog's maximum range was a hundred yards or so, and then only in pursuit of rabbits. When Clifford went to Ripley, to borrow a variety of carpentry tools, Puffin and Dusty accompanied him.

From day one at the cabin Puffin had been essentially Clifford's terrier, a fact he displayed by greeting Monica's spaniels when he happened to meet them, courteously, but not effusively, and treating Mrs Harris, the housekeeper, with some disdain. When Clifford made expeditions to Tillston he was reluctant to take Dusty with him. He had become so fond of the lurcher, which increasingly reminded him of the lamented Snakey, that he was worried that someone there might see him and claim him. Of course Clifford hadn't the least idea of the kind of life Dusty had previously endured, but he didn't like the smell of the dog at first. It had the aura of having come from an evil place. Anyhow, for him, a dog should be where a dog was happiest, never mind the true owner's concern. And Dusty couldn't possibly be happier elsewhere.

Because he didn't want to leave Dusty behind, alone, on his trips to Tillston he no longer took Puffin there either. He was obliged to shut them up in the cabin to stop them following him to the village on the second morning after Dusty's arrival. But the next time Clifford set off for supplies, they got the message. He had an unusual way with dogs and persuaded them to stay put without locking them up. But not for long.

By midday when he returned laden with more planks

of wood, a tin of creosote and a bag of cement, his dogs were not at home. Mystified, he stood by the pond and called and waited, but there was no sign of them. He left the rhododendron enclave and called again. Still no Puffin, no Dusty. He walked down the forest ride that crossed the public footpath, his original route to Ripley. And at last he saw them in the oak wood to the left, half hidden by trees, their whole attention arrested by something beyond. He called *'Here, Puffin! Come, both of you!'* They looked up for a second, then gazed back in the opposite direction.

When Clifford was within forty yards of them he caught a fleeting glimpse of an animal half-a-dozen oaks away, a grey shadowy figure. He quickened his pace for a closer look, a glimpse that was to give him a strange sense of foreboding. Was it a German shepherd, an alsatian type? He advanced a few paces. No, not really. It was brownish grey with smaller ears and longer, straighter legs than an alsatian. Its eyes were yellow and narrow and slightly slanting, with the most malevolent look he had ever seen in a dog. Its ribs showed starkly through its coarse grey-brown coat. Now the yellow eyes met his own and, in a flash, the creature retreated deeper into the forest, tail sunk, ears flattened. *So that is the source of the desolate, wavering howl we've been hearing in the night!*

Puffin and Dusty started to follow the creature, but Clifford called them again and this time they came to him, heads held low, looking guilty and apologetic. He imagined that there was only one temptation that would have lured them from the cabin, only one reason why they'd ignored his initial calls. The baleful looking wolf-type must be a bitch on heat, probably hungry as well as lustful. The expression in those yellow eyes had sent a little shiver down Clifford's spine, which repeated itself as he returned to the cabin. 'Now, Puffin,' he muttered, 'you just forget about that bitch!.'

Rounding the corner of the rhododendron entrance to the cabin enclave he was met by another sight that was not altogether welcome. Standing on the verandah, hands resting on its rail, was a figure in a black suit and a clerical dog collar. 'Oh hell,' thought Clifford, 'Monica's brother . . .'

III

'Good morning! Mr Clifford, I presume? And that must be Monica's Puffin with you, no? Awful little yapper. I'm Richard Illingworth. Monica asked me to call on you,'

Clifford surveyed his visitor, a corpulent figure with fastidious face and podgy hands, a man who looked quite out of place in the depths of this woodland. He shook the vicar's proffered hand. 'Yes, this is Puffin,' he said, then pointed to Dusty. 'But you wouldn't know that one. It's a stray that got bumped into by a car just outside Tillston,'

The Rev Richard glanced with cold disdain at both dogs. 'What a lot of trouble pets give. Quite honestly, you know, society would be far better off without them altogether. I had Puffin's mother with me until she ran away and gave me a lot of trouble. That put me off dogs forever. There are far too many people taking pity on strays and other creatures. If only they'd concentrate their energies on their less fortunate *brethren*.'

''Fraid I can't agree with that, Mr Illingworth.'

'Plus que je vois les hommes, plus que j'aime les chiens.' I suppose you go along with that? Attributed to Voltaire, but really Madame de Sévigné, I believe. Terrible people those French 18th century intellectuals.'

Irritated by the man's showing off, Clifford shrugged

and glanced at his watch. He hesitated. He wanted to get on with the repairs; at the same time he felt he should spare a bit of courtesy for his hostess's brother. 'Come along into the cabin, Mr Illingworth, and let me give you a glass of sherry.'

'Oh, thank you, that would be nice.' The vicar inclined his bald head with an ingratiating smile.

Clifford took a couple of tin mugs from a shelf, poured a small measure of sherry into each and waved his visitor towards a chair. Then he opened a tin of dogmeat into Snakey's bowl for Dusty, who ate it up in a few gulps.

Illingworth, eyeing the tin mug with unconcealed disdain, cleared his throat and looked benign. 'I understand, Mr Clifford, that you've had the misfortune to lose your wife recently?'

Jack felt his body go tense. 'Yes, I did,' he replied crisply, 'that is really why I'm here.'

'Well I had the satisfaction of giving dear Monica some counsel and comfort after Edward Bowes-Onslow died and we thought ... well we thought you might like to chat about *your* sorrow, too.'

'I wish to do no such thing,' said Jack. 'But thank you all the same.'

'I'm very experienced in these matters, I could help, you know.'

'Frankly, I don't wish to be reminded, it would be opening up a very deep wound, I have mourned long enough ... Incidentally, my own dog was killed when I first arrived here. I'm still upset about that.'

Illingworth took out a handkerchief and, wiping his glasses, slowly shook his head. 'Oh, I'm sorry to say it, but I wish people wouldn't concern themselves with the death of animals. It's immoral. Mourning should be confined to the human race'. He looked towards the dogs. 'They are dirty in the eyes of our Maker, and wasteful of men's time.'

'Once again, I don't agree with you. Every loss of life saddens me.'

'That — I'm sorry to say it — is sheer sentimentality.'

'To me, an animal's suffering, according to the degree of it, is just as serious in the eyes of God as a human's.'

Illingworth opened his mouth with a sharp intake of breath. 'It is surely sacrilege to say that.'

Clifford sighed impatiently. 'Well, that's my belief. Furthermore, I think your religion has always been mistaken for putting the human race on a higher plane than God's creatures and plants. This morning I stood with a woman lamenting the rape of an old forest near here, a woodland of deciduous trees being taken out to make way for a conifer plantation. That's my idea of sacrilege. If the time ever comes when strong and genuine voices are heard from the church about the salvation of animals and the conservation of wildlife, then Christianity might be taken more seriously again. And another thing . . .' But there Clifford broke off and, raising his eyes to the cabin's ceiling, he frowned, listening carefully. The silence had been broken by shots, very distant shots. 'Gunfire,' he said, 'I wonder where that's coming from?'

The vicar heard it, too. 'That'll be the Leawood shoot, the first of the season I should think. Young Nigel Harrington runs it now. I officiated when he married his pretty bride, Sarah, Monica's daughter, just the other day. They're a sweet young couple. I adore my niece.'

'Your Nigel Harrington can't be that sweet if he enjoys killing things.'

'Oh I don't know, Mr Clifford. For those people shooting's a healthy diversion. Not only gives them fresh air and exercise but gets the violence out of them. I know I'm being a bit cynical when I say this — but otherwise they'd probably be damaging *people*.'

'No comment,' said Clifford.

Illingworth rose to go. 'Well, there we are, we must agree to differ. It doesn't look as though we're going to find any common ground this morning.' The vicar gave him a patronising grin. When they were on the verandah he put out his hand again and shook Clifford's. 'I hope you enjoy your time in the cabin. If you change your mind and would like my help you can always leave a message with Mrs Harris.'

'Thank you,' *The man means well*, thought Clifford, watching the black retreating figure move through the compound's rhododendron passage. Then he turned his attention to Dusty. He picked up Snakey's brush and started grooming the Sewells' injured dog and went on brushing for six or seven minutes while Puffin lay in his habitual pose of concentrated interest. ... *well now, Puffin, what are we going to call our visitor? We must give him a name even if we find we've got to surrender him tomorrow. We can't have an anonymous guest can we, Puff? I'm tempted to have him as Snakey the second, this being the split image. But no ... there was really only one Snakey. Just look at the gloss on his coat now, Puffin. And you remember his dowdy look? And how about the new sparkle in those eyes? Brilliant, eh? Brilliant yes, that's the name for him, Brill for short. How d'you like that, Brill?* And Brill put his head between Clifford's hands and whined ecstatically. Clifford paused and listened again. The shooting had stopped. The end of a drive, he supposed; they were knocking off for lunch perhaps. Then he heard something else. It was that long eerie howling, very distant now, only faintly audible. The animal in the woods. And he saw that both dogs had their hackles up.

Sarah Harrington clapped her mittened hands. 'Well done, Nige!' she cried. It was the penultimate drive of the first day's shooting of the season and another high pheasant had fallen to her husband's gun. With his tall lean straight backed figure, dressed in tweed knickerbockers, cap and waxed jacket, he seemed to his newly-wed wife, who sat on a shooting stick just behind him, to be the epitome of all that was right and smart and good and healthy for an autumn day in the country. Nigel Harrington was a game-shot who took immense pride in dispatching his birds cleanly.

Much pride, too, in his working dogs. This young labrador of his, Zebedee, showed great promise, always marking, finding and retrieving the birds he shot with faithful precision and no undue delay, although the dog had barely completed its training. Not bad for a labrador not yet two years old, he decided.

It was a crisp sunny afternoon with the leaves damp from the now-melted frost of the previous night, the sun glinting through the branches and a sharp enticing forest odour on the air. Nigel, who had recently taken over the running of the Leawood shoot from his father (though his father still had charge of the keepering) was proud of the way the opening day had gone; proud of the sport he had provided for the syndicate guns; proud of his beautiful Sarah who had charmed them all and laid on such a splendid buffet lunch in the old barn; and, not least, proud of his young labrador, Zebedee, who was retrieving like a veteran. As he slung his cartridge bag over his shoulder to proceed with the other seven guns to the positions for the last drive, pretty Sarah spoke again. 'Oh hell, there's Mr Jarrow pointing in our direction,' she pouted, 'He me no like.'

Nigel watched the keeper, accompanied by a cowed looking springer spaniel on a very short lead, approach their stand. *Jarrow's one of those men who . . . well, you never quite know where you were with,* thought Nigel, *a sycophantic fellow, but one who probably has something quite different to say behind your back. Not entirely trustworthy in his job either. I'd really like to get rid of him. Trouble is father wouldn't allow it . . .*

'Your young labrador's picking up well, sir,' said Jarrow touching his deerstalker hat. Dressed in a three-piece checkered knickerbocker suit he was a thin, heavy-lidded man with a stoop and a downward curl on the corners of his lips. 'I don't think I've ever seen a dog bring in the birds quicker.'

'Oh thank you,' said Nigel recognizing, and shrinking from, the unctuous flattery, 'I'll pass on the compliment. Yes, Zebedee's a marvel for a young dog. All done by kindness. And we've got plenty of birds to show. Flying well, too.'

'Ay we have, we have that,' said Jarrow smugly. 'What's your number for the last drive?'

'Five.'

'Ah, you'll be in the hot seat then. You'll be right on the footpath in front of the Temple. The best of 'em usually fly over that point. Er . . . but you'll need to take them in front, they drop very quickly behind just there . . . going down over the brook that is and onto the Ripley land. There must be hundreds of our birds there,' the keeper added, shaking his head ruefully.

'Well, you certainly manage to rear and bring on plenty,' said Nigel briskly.

'I never got rid of more vermin than I have this year,' Jarrow grinned. 'More'n any other shoot in the south of England I'll bet. Magpies, jays, crows, squirrels — ay and foxes by the hundred — you name the buggers I've clobbered 'em. If any keeper claims more 'n me I'd like to hear from 'em.'

'Ah, now this is something I've never asked you: what's your anti-predator secret — the usual, I suppose, shooting and trapping?'

'The usual, sir — and poison.'

Nigel regarded his father's employee closely. 'I didn't know you put poison down. Aren't all the poisons illegal now? What d'you use?'

'I put strychnine in me baits.'

Nigel grimaced. 'Strychnine? That's the worst of them all. I think you'd better stop doing that.'

Jarrow gave him a cold double take. 'Your father approves, never mind the law. What's good enough for Mr Harrington is good enough for me and ought to be good enough for you, I reckon.'

'Well it isn't good enough. I'll speak to my father about it.'

At that the keeper strode away without another word, but with an impertinent toss of the head. And Sarah, watching him go, said 'Oh Nige, he's odious, you've got to get rid of him.'

'He's father's man, not mine.'

Ten minutes later the guns were standing by their pegs for the last drive. Nigel turned, for a moment, from Rockingham copse to look behind him to the ring of beeches enclosing the replica of a Greek temple with its surround of stone goddesses. And very fine they looked, too, he thought, reflecting the gold from the setting sun.

'Who built that?' Sarah wanted to know.

'My grandfather,' Nigel told her. 'He was an eccentric who forbade any killing by human hand on the estate. He was reputed to have evicted a tenant for throwing a boot at a cat and, on another occasion, so rumour had it, sacked his forester for shooting a hawk.'

'M'm — quite a contrast to your old father.'

'You could say that . . . oh God, Sarah, you're pretty! Can I kiss you?'

'No no, not now darling; your father's heading in this

direction, looking grim, too.'

Edwin Harrington was a stout man with a florid, expensive-looking face and a black moustache which he was now tugging at rather angrily. 'Well Nigel, long wait here, eh?'

'That's right, usually takes the beaters about ten minutes to get into position at the far end of Rockingham,' his son replied.

'That's just why I took the opportunity of having a word with you. Jarrow's been complaining to me about you lecturing him on how to control his vermin.'

'I wouldn't have called it lecturing, Dad, just objecting to him using such illegal measures as strychnine and gin traps. I don't mind how many vermin he destroys as long as he does it humanely. All I want . . .'

'Now you just stick to running the day's sport' — Edwin Harrington raised his voice and hammered the point of his shooting-stick into the ground. 'You leave Jarrow to keep down the predators in his own way, d'you hear? You leave his work to me, he's my business . . .' And with those words Nigel's father returned to his stand.

'Well. *really,* what a man!' - Sarah spat her objection at her father-in-law's back — 'He didn't even look at me, let alone give me a smile.'

'I'll make up for it,' promised Nigel, 'now I'm going to have that kiss!'

'No you're not — look out, pheasant over!'

Nigel swung onto his birds with that same prompt yet easy style and he reloaded quick as a conjuror. Every pheasant that came within range of his unerring barrels crumpled and spiralled onto the turf with a soft, stone-dead thump. Zebedee whined deliriously, but remained sitting obediently at his master's side. It was a long thick wood; the beaters were nearly twenty minutes working their way through it.

'Go on, Zebedee, fetch!' Nigel ordered as the beaters emerged. And the dog, with feverish concentration and hyperactivity, began bringing in his pheasants, until twelve were counted. But Nigel remembered a cock bird that had flown from left to right and which he'd taken well forward to drop inside the covert. He signalled Zebedee on again and the eager labrador, his healthy black coat shining like broken coals, romped over the ditch and barbed wire which enclosed the copse and began searching excitedly amongst the briar and bramble undergrowth.

'Is that all?' asked one of the two beaters who approached to collect the birds.

'Thank you — yes, all except a cock inside the covert, my dog's fetching it now.'

At last Zebedee scented the big russet, green and tawny bird. A few moments later he spotted it, caught six feet up, in the fork of a sapling. With sinuous, athletic leaps he jumped for it several times, but his teeth failed to connect. Thus thwarted he stood at the bottom, craning, waving his tail agitatedly and squealing. After thirty seconds or so of that his black wet nostrils received another scent, a quite different scent, which suddenly sent a wave of wonder and excitement through his whole frame, which prompted him to forget the bird and find the source. For that he had only to run a half-circle.

What he saw inflamed him more. His pelt bristled, his tail wagged, his brow puckered, his eyes gleamed, his tongue lolled, his loins thrilled, his voice whimpered. Ten yards away stood a dog with lowered head, twitching nose and rigid posture, a dog of about his own size, of the general conformation of a German shepherd, but grey-brown, yellow-eyed, a bit longer in the leg and with smaller ears than an alsatian, a dog that must have followed the beaters into the covert in the hope of food. Not that Zebedee could compare it comprehensively with

other dogs for, close-to, he had only met breeds trained for the gun like himself and the only one of those he knew well was old Bongo, his retired sire, with whom he shared a kennel. Anyhow its visual appearance was neither here nor there, it was the creature's harbinger, her odour, that mattered.

Zebedee's brain registered Nigel's whistle, but all his other senses ignored it. He heard *Zebedee! Zebedee! Come on boy — what are you up to in there?* But his libido predominated. Nigel's command, hitherto the only real imperative in his life, held no importance for him at this moment. The labrador was hypnotised by the creature whose glands gave off this heavenly redolence. He could only respond to this gloriously unfamiliar, irresistible lure. The wolf-like bitch withdrew a few paces, stopped, looked over her shoulder to see if he was following and repeated the act until they were both clear of the wood and descending the hill. *Zebedee! Zebedee!* came Nigel's faintly echoing voice, but the labrador — attention still utterly riveted on his new companion — could only disregard it. He followed the bitch's every twist and turn, taking the greatest interest in every place where she urinated, which she did frequently, but only to dispose of an enticing drop or two each time.

Just short of the footbridge that carried the path over the stream onto the Ripley estate, the bitch stopped to inspect a dead rabbit that had been slit down its front. Her nose warned her against the acrid smell, the gamekeeper's poison, that came from its stomach and she left it. When she reached the top of the hill beyond the bridge, a short distance from where Clifford had buried Snakey, she stopped, turned and walked back to Zebedee who had been following nervously, but still very eagerly, some ten yards behind her. She sniffed him back and front and after he had returned the enquiry — young frightened innocent that he was — he rolled on his back. With a movement of obvious impatience, the bitch, now at the climax of her season, presented herself. And Zebedee having licked her coat, then her genitals, mounted her. As soon as they were disengaged from their mutually ecstatic tie, which endured — with their heads pointing in different directions — for fifteen minutes, the bitch, all passion spent, led her mate unhesitatingly to the summer-house in the rhododendron grove — the building where she had been finding scraps of food — while Zebedee kept nosing her over her neck and shoulders as she trotted along the footpath.

An hour had passed since their encounter in Pheasant copse. When Clifford found them they were lying together beyond the lily pond, wholly relaxed with tongue-lolling, lazy-eye gratified faces, obviously blissful in one another's company. *That wolf-like bitch again — with a labrador! They must have just copulated* which, he presumed, *is why she's softened in this way. So, hopefully, her season will soon be over. But why did she lead her paramour here? Because there was a smell of food.* He looked at them again, the labrador so sleek, the bitch so thin. He took pity on her. He would give her a name. She was so like a wolf, he would call her Lupus. No — Lupa. He climbed the cabin steps, went into the little building, ordered Puffin and Brill to sit still, mixed some meal and milk in Puffin's bowl and, closing the door behind him, went to give it to Lupa. But, by the time he returned, she was gone. There was only the labrador sniffing at the spot where she had lain. So Clifford put the bowl down for this new intruder and examined its collar while it ate. No identification there. His fingers felt through Zebedee's glossy black coat while he took note of the alert eyes and wet nose. And also of the unusual white tip on the tail. *A well kept healthy dog. But it can't stay here, that's for* certain, he decided. *Well, just for tonight, perhaps . . . It'd better come indoors, keep it out of mischief.* And Zebedee, eye still half on the empty food bowl, followed Clifford into the cabin where the other dogs approached him with suspicious enquiry.

Here, labrador, you must watch your step with little Puffin, because he's top dog, Clifford's unspoken thoughts went on. *Talking of top dogs you've just been Lupa's shadow haven't you, her instrument, nothing more . . .? Anyhow, you'll not be here long enough for me to bother naming you. Tomorrow we must find your owner.*

Next morning, having walked Brill and Zebedee and then shut them in the house, Clifford, still accompanied by Puffin, set out for Tillston police station where he told the sergeant about Zebedee. The sergeant glanced at his records and replied that no dog of that description had been reported. Five minutes after Clifford left the village, the sergeant mentioned his visit to a constable arriving on duty. This constable said that 'young Nigel Harrington from Leawood' had called in the previous evening and reported the loss of his black labrador and was offering a large reward. The sergeant asked the constable why he hadn't recorded the matter. To which the junior declared that having 'a lot on his mind at the time he quite forgot.' The sergeant replied, not without asperity, that 'the bloke who called this morning gave his name as John Clifford, but of no fixed address. You'd better keep your eyes skinned for him.'

Meanwhile, Clifford had another change of heart. He no sooner made a resolution to telephone the nearest dog shelter and arrange for Brill and Zebedee to be collected than he changed his mind. He had heard too many bad accounts of so-called animal sanctuaries. So he compromised by promising himself that no more dogs would be allowed near — so long as he occupied the cabin. But, even on that, he was to relent.

IV

The beagles were the only canines at the Barberry research station that autumn. There were some cats, three monkeys, a few guinea pigs and a great many white rats and mice, but only those two dogs. Having been bred expressly for experimentation the beagles had known no other life than that of the clinical laboratory, an existence that might, to the average animal lover, seem unremittingly bleak and bland, and often painful. Yet their noses were invariably wet and their coats glossy, and they always wagged their tails ecstatically at the approach of the nice girl who fed and exercised them, brushed them, kept them free from flea and worm, and loved them.

Nor did they mind the intermittent inspections and handling by the white-coated men with earnest expressions, tight smiles and knitted brows. They had been accustomed to that treatment since puppyhood. Such experiments as they endured from time to time were always carried out under a full anaesthetic and they were manipulated as humanely as possible in the course of the various operations to which they owed their very being. Although there would often be some discomfort during recovery, it was far from intolerable. The Barberry scientists asserted that vivisection had saved many lives and much suffering, of animals as well as people, and would continue to do so; and that animal welfarist sentimentality was both silly and illogical.

At the time of the opening of the great drama of those dogs' lives they had just got over a brain test, involving the insertion of electrodes in the top of their skulls, the instruments having been removed about four weeks previously. Both beagles occasionally made gestures with their paws as though they could still feel the weight of the gadgets, but there was no trace left except where the hair had not fully grown out and the white scars showing where the instruments had been fixed. Theirs was a fairly monotonous mode of living — compared with that of, say, Puffin and Brill and Zebedee in their present circumstances — but it was by no means a miserable one. Above all they enjoyed security, the comforting assurance that they were wanted and loved. That was their situation until the night of their 'freedom', an early November night which began with the moon high up in the sky.

Those intervening in the dogs' lives comprised a gang of three, two young men and a woman. The first the beagles knew of them was to see, quite suddenly out of the darkness of the laboratory, flashes of torchlight around the kennel and cage area that was their home, then torchlight in their eyes.

'Quick, Michael — Here, Jimmy!' The young woman's voice hissed. 'I've found a couple of dogs!' She was adorned in black from head to foot, black turtle neck sweater, black tight trousers, black trainers, a black band holding back her yellow hair.

'Good, those'll do, won't they?' whispered the one called Jimmy, who wore a balaclava. 'Both male, are they, Janet?' The slippery, whispery chorus of their three pairs of trainers squeaked on the stone floor.

'Yes they are, take one each!' snapped Janet, and the beagles, too frightened to resist, were lifted, squealing their protest, into the embrace of strong young male arms.

'Come on then!' she ordered, 'we'll get out the way we came!'.

'Have you left the SEEA message?' asked Michael, a youth with a wispy beard and a pony tail of hair jutting out from beneath his woollen cap.

'I'm leaving it now.' she replied, dropping on the kennel floor two leaflets entitled 'the Declaration of the Society for the Elimination of the Exploitation of Animals'. 'Come on then, let's go!' Leading the way with her torch, and closely followed by her male confederates carrying the bewildered beagles, she stalked along the corridors, flitted like some reincarnation of Batman down the stairs, and led the way out of the ground floor window, which they had broken to enter the building.

Suddenly floodlight was added to the moonlight on the lawns beyond. 'Oh, shit, there's an alarm going — the bastards!' Janet spat the words as she landed from the window onto the paving below. 'Hurry up with those bloody dogs you lot!'

'Bloke coming over from the left,' added Michael, 'look out Janet!'

'Night watchman, I suppose, let's make a dash for it! .'

The beagles shivered now — from the November air as well as from fear — and began to struggle as they were carried at a run across the adjoining lawns.

'Hey there, where the hell do you think you're going with them?' yelled the laboratory man doubling and puffing towards the raiders' waiting van. He closed in on them just as they were opening the doors, but receiving a strong blow on the jaw from Michael, who had transferred his charge to beneath his left arm, the man went reeling across the grass. Within less than two minutes of leaving the building, the beagles found themselves bundled onto the back seat of the van. 'Any more sign of alarm from the laboratory?' Janet asked across her shoulder as she started up.

'Not a murmur and the bell's stopped now.' Jimmy took off his balaclava.

'Bloke's still rubbing his interfering face,' said Michael.

'Right. Good.' Janet accelerated down the drive, and flung a message to the dogs. 'We've liberated you two, did you know that, darlings? No more torture, no more butchery, now you can do your own thing, we're going to release you onto the big wide free world. You've been freed by the heroes of SEEA. Aren't you lucky little doggies then, eh?'

The beagles, in response, continued to cower and shiver on the seat between the two men. They had never, in all their lives, suffered such a terrifying experience. Their staring eyes showed their terror.

'Oughtn't we to give 'em a home, I mean look out some owners for them?' Michael suggested.

Janet gritted her teeth as she raced from Hampshire towards Wiltshire, heading due west, 'Good idea in principle, trouble is the police might trace us if we did that. The police are on the side of the torturers. Don't you forget that! And the law doesn't listen to reason when it come to humaneness.'

'That's right', Jimmy agreed. 'Besides, the dogs don't want to be shut up with some owner who might not be much better than the Barberry research people. And another thing, Michael,' he added with light sarcasm, 'you don't need reminding that our Janet went to college, with a degree in zoology no less. There are no spots on her!'

'All right, you win. But who'll feed them and that if we just drop them?'

'Dogs learn to live off the country soon enough,' said Janet with her voice of rational authority. 'They'll go back to nature like wild dogs, they'll just do as nature intended. That's what our organisation's about isn't it, setting animals free?'

Cloud had obscured the moon. Now there was darker cloud and a distant rumble of thunder, and the rain started. Janet switched the windscreen wiper to fast.

'These look as though they could be beagles', Michael remarked. 'You know what they're bred for? Hunting and killing hares. You know what they do? They tear the animal limb from limb while it screams in agony and the hunters stand round cheering and laughing.'

'They're devils those hunters.'

Jimmy had been busy inspecting the beagles with his torch. 'God, you should see this, they've got scars right on the top of their heads as though they've had nails hammered in there or something. They're both shivering in agony from the torture. It's disgusting!'

'*What?* I can hardly believe it! Those scientists are right bastards and no mistake. What would you do if we got our hands on them — no, don't bother answering that, boys . . . But, honestly, those bastards must be devoid of any feeling. Vivisection indeed — what a euphemism. Deliberate, calculated invasion of animal rights, that's what I call it, nothing less than anti-animal terrorism . . .'

'Here, what about this black wood looming up on the left, Janet?' Jimmy interrupted her, 'they'll have shelter there.'

'OK, might as well be here as anywhere.' She pulled into a forestry entrance. 'I should carry them through that gate and put them in amongst the trees, boys — well away from the road. They'll be safe as houses in there.'

The two men dragged the beagles from the van by the scruffs of their necks, then pulled them at a reluctant walk through the gate in the fence enclosing the woodland and so to the cover of the trees, where the dogs set up a miserable whining duet under the fast falling rain.

'. . . Well, that's that,' said Michael shaking off

raindrops as he climbed back into the car. 'Now we can really start congratulating ourselves. I wonder if it'll be in the morning papers.'

'No, but it'll be on the radio — and in the papers the morning after. Lovely publicity for SEEA. Those dogs'll love the rain on their backs, probably never felt it before.'

'Lovely for the dogs, lovely for us, lovely for the Society for the Elimination of the Exploitation of Animals.'

'Let's have the SEEA song then,' suggested Janet as she let in the clutch and turned onto the road again. And the words of the raucous lilt, of which the beagles heard the first bar or two as they cringed in the black wood, rang out in the night air: *See-a, See-a, we save the animals from fee-ar, fee-ar. See-a, See-a, we save the animals from fee-ar!* The three 'rescuers' continued their song with triumph in their throats, but before the repetition of that opening line their voices had faded on the road and the beagles were left with nothing but the silence of the forest, broken only by the awesome whistle of the wind through the alien trees that served for scant shelter. It rained relentlessly till dawn.

The beagles didn't roam during the night, but crouched, shivering, under the dripping trees. In the morning they sought the light of a forest ride where — while the sun rose and they felt its friendly, if thin, warmth on their backs — their noses, coupled with their homing instinct, dictated their movement. This total contrast — to the unnatural environment in which they had languished from the time they left their dam's womb until now — brought many contradictions to noses that had known little else other than the hygienic laboratorial stench, or the scents of the manicured lawns and footpaths outside the research station. Fascinated by the novel, odorous experiences of farmyard and plough, streamside and tarmac, copse and hedgerow, they wandered on through the day.

Above all such diversions a stronger instinct prevailed, one that impelled them towards that point of the compass from which the SEEA people's car had driven them. But while, in general, they pointed their heads in that direction they also stopped every so often to savour this particular fragrance, or to cock their ears at that absorbing high-pitched animal sound. They were not unduly hungry in the morning. So moving eastwards without urgency, they raised a leg against a post here, snuffled at some toadstools there, rolled in rabbit droppings, barked up a tree scaled by a squirrel, or scratched with their hind claws at a carpet of wet coppery leaves, marking their route automatically as nature dictated.

Since they found nothing to assuage the hunger pangs that set in during the afternoon they continued to trot along in this meandering way, but always on the magnetic bearing that might eventually have led them back to Barberry. However, a little before the sun began to sink behind them, as they trotted alongside a conifer plantation, they sniffed out an aroma so potently enchanting that they found all their senses, so to speak, in bondage to it. To them it was like nectar to the gods; they were drawn towards it as a thirsty human on a parched desert trek might be drawn towards the smell of water. This fragrance, dispelling the recent imperative of hunger, filled their loins with mysterious joy.

And, after about ten minutes, they saw the subject of it. Forty yards away a big lean grey-brown dog with a lupine head, short ears and yellow eyes, stood stock still staring back at them. Then it moved on; but, every thirty or forty yards, it stopped and turned again as though to confirm for itself that its delicious scent still held them in thrall. For the beagles, all feeling of weariness lifted.

They licked their chops, they whined, they scratched the leaves and the grass, and they pricked up their ears as they advanced irresistibly in the wake of this ever-retreating wolf dog. Nothing in their previous existence had ever thrilled them even half as much as this.

At last the bitch led them to a great thicket of rhododendron through which a narrow avenue had been cut. As it lured them onto this path a trio of barking arose, one voice being the yap of a terrier, the others deeper sounds of larger dogs. The temptress sidled round the inside perimeter of the clearing within the rhododendrons, while the beagles, distracted for the moment by the barking, advanced cautiously towards the wooden building that marked the centre of it in the place where the bitch had, from time to time, been finding scraps of food.

The sun on the beagles' first day on the loose was sinking now, and Clifford, roused from his book by Puffin, Brill and Zebedee giving riotous tongue from the verandah, went out to see what had excited them. Nosing towards him, licking their muzzles and swinging their sterns in hesitant greeting, were two beagles, well-fed looking dogs. The three cabin dogs looked past them and, hackles up, lips curled, barked furiously. Then Clifford, hearing a whimper by the enclosure wall of rhododendrons, turned in that direction. The wolf-like bitch gave him one hard look accompanied by a little yelp, then scurried away towards the entrance. Clifford was beginning to regret having put food down for the bitch. 'A-argh, go away you *Lupa!*' he shouted. 'Yes, *Lupa because you look more like a wolf than anything I've ever set eyes on outside a zoo. Wretched creature coming into season just when I happen to be here!*'

Clifford murmured this last sentiment as he went indoors, where Puffin, Zebedee and Brill were busy examining the two newcomers, front and rear. 'Come away, Puff, let me have a look, too,' he said drawing one of the beagles towards him. *M'm, both boys.* Finding the scars on top of their heads he realised that they had been, at one time or another, in an experimental laboratory. He pondered, stroked his chin thoughtfully, then ran his fingers through the fur of the revealing places. His moral sense had told him, in the cases of Brill and Zebedee, that, as a good citizen, he ought to inform the police and see these dogs returned from where they had come. But vivisection was something he harboured strong feelings about. He'd always hated everything he'd heard about animal experimentation, whether it was on mice or monkeys. *They could have been let loose by animal rights people,* he conjectured, *the sort of nutters that burn butchers' shops or pull down mink farm fences and let those vandals free on the countryside.*

All the same, if he owned up to these beagles being here they'd be returned to the hell of the laboratory. Or possibly they were only former laboratory inmates that had somehow found their way into private hands? In that case they'd be committed, likely as not, to some run-down animal shelter with only a faint prospect of ending up in a kind home. The alternative is to keep them here. After all, I can't send them away to starve. Why not keep them — for the moment? Yes — I'll let them stay for the time being and see what happens. Like Brill and Zebedee they might be claimed and they might not. It had been borne in on him ever since he'd buried Snakey, that his attitude to life was increasingly one of procrastination, and he didn't much like himself for it. *Is it my unreliable heart that prompts this sentiment, he wondered, a feeling that my days are closely numbered? That by putting off decisions I can put off death?* Then he told himself to stop worrying. He'd suffered no chest pains since he'd been at the cabin. But the anxiety nagged all the same.

The beagles slipped from Clifford's fingers to exchange sniffing messages with Brill and Zebedee; and Puffin hopped onto his knees. *Come to think of it he wasn't at all sure what to do with himself, let alone all these animals, for that matter. He supposed he'd stay on until Monica Bowes-Onslow returned, then make his way home — though he didn't anticipate this with any great relish going back to that lonely house by Beachy Head, once so bright and happy, but utterly bleak since Kate's death. As he retraced his steps for home, would he have these five newly-found dogs at heel, where — setting out — there had just been Snakey? What a bizarre thought. No, not five surely — just Puffin. The rest must be disposed of . . .*

He watched the beagles sniffing at the shelves where he kept the dog food and wondered how long they'd gone hungry. He opened a tin, half-boiled a kettle, mixed the meat and warm water with some meal, and filled two bowls. They were ravenous. While they ate he lit the four lamps, then cast an eye around the little summer house with a nod of satisfaction. He was pleased with the way the stain he'd used on those new floorboards had blended so well with the old. Yes, and the window-frames, which fitted like a glove now, looked really good with their fresh paint; the polycarbonate plastic he used for the panes would be much more suitable for a place like this than the glass which had given way to them; and that patch of hitherto leaking roof had withstood the heavy showers of two nights ago. The next thing to put right was the curtain rails; then he'd have some curtains measured up.

He took a torch and, followed by Puffin, wandered onto the verandah. He pushed against the top rail and the two posts he'd inserted earlier in the day. *They didn't give an inch. Good* . . . Puffin suddenly began yapping very urgently. Clifford swung the torch onto him. The terrier's hackles were up. He switched the beam to the left side of the lily pond, than to the right. It lit up that menacing pair of eyes again, those narrow eyes and the large shadowy form behind them. The inscrutable Lupa. Still held in Clifford's torchlight, the wolf-like dog advanced until she was only ten yards from the verandah steps. Racing forward, Puffin hurled himself at her head and, so far as Clifford could see, bit her on the ear. With a yelp she turned tail and ran for the rhododendron entrance lane.

Brill, Zebedee and the beagles, who had been barking from the verandah, rushed down to snuffle eagerly over every inch she'd traversed. So eagerly that Clifford knew she must be very much still on heat. *Probably starving, poor thing,* he thought, half relenting again. *Still, I can't add a bitch to the pack, least of all that sinister creature.*

Puffin was standing guard at the entrance path, barking. 'Here, come on back, Puff! Good boy!' *You won't let anyone come onto our patch without permission will you? Quite right, Puff.* But, like the others, faithful Puffin couldn't resist the fragrance the bitch stranger left behind. He sniffed at the places where she'd lingered with at least as much enthusiasm as the other four dogs before following his master indoors. Clifford looked at Zebedee and thought: *funny things dogs, here's a labrador that was intimate with that bitch only yesterday, but all he does now is bark at her. Yes — very odd creatures. He wouldn't name Zebedee; it might give the labrador some claim on him. Whereas he wanted someone else to claim him, the sooner the better.*

Mrs Harris, arriving next morning with a small shopping bag of apples and pears from the Ripley orchard, found Clifford concentrating deeply on a sketch of the beagles. Knowing and trusting her, Puffin went up with a jaunty greeting, jerking his white stump of a tail. Zebedee ignored her. Brill, who'd only met her once — and was anyway still in a timid mood from his trauma — advanced more cautiously. The beagles, exhausted from their travels, simply raised and lowered their heads. Mrs Harris took off her rimless glasses, wiped them on her coat and, narrowing her eyes at the artist's models, replaced them carefully on the bridge of her puffy nose. 'More dogs, Mr Clifford?' she exclaimed, 'you'll have a hunting pack soon!'

'They're strays, needless to say.' He stopped work for a moment, gave Mrs Harris a welcoming smile, then focussed on the beagles again, speaking as he sketched. 'There's a big wild creature, a bitch, hovering around the wood looking for food which she smells here. In fact she's had two bowls of our dog food already, which I left out by mistake. She's on heat; I reckon she guided them here. She almost certainly mated with that black labrador. I call her Lupa, from Lupus, wolf. Do you know about her?'

'Can't say I do, though I have heard a funny howling of a night-time. Given me the shivers it has, not to mention starting our spaniels barking and waking me up,' replied Mrs Harris abstractedly. Then turning her attention to the five dogs in the room: 'Are you going to keep all this lot then? Well, Puffin, of course. But Mrs Bowes-Onslow won't like this many wandering round here.'

'I haven't decided. Puffin's mine, of course, and I think I'll be able to dispose of the others.'

'It'd be just as well if you do, if I may say so.'

Without raising his eyes from the beagles Clifford made a gesture of impatience. 'I'll play it off the cuff. I'm sure the labrador'll be claimed and I think the lurcher's got a good home to go to. I don't know about the beagles.'

'Anyhow I've brought some nice ripe fruit for you.'

'Thank you very much, Mrs Harris.'

'Can I have a look at your drawing?'

'Yes, do if you like.'

She walked round behind him, paused, then said 'oh nice, very nice. You've got them to a T. Have you given them names?'

Clifford's pencil hovered over his sketch. He turned to her, laughing warmly by this time. 'Yes — seeing they're beagles I've called them Seagull and Regal to rhyme. Easy to remember which from t'other that way.'

'That's clever!' she returned his laugh, then suddenly went solemn. 'Oh, I've had a thought.'

'What's that?' Clifford's pencil was correcting his foreshortening of Seagull's forepaw where it rested beneath the beagle's muzzle.

'Well, when I tuned into the local radio early there was something about a laboratory being broken into and two beagles stolen the night before last. Animal Rights people, the announcer said. They left leaflets behind about themselves. They were the — wait a minute — yes, the Society for the Elimination ... of the Exploitation of Animals — SEEA, that's it ... Oh Mr Clifford, you say this pair turned up yesterday evening?'

Clifford felt his heart beat a little faster, and the old pain was there. *I've grown quite fond of these little dogs already,* he realised. *It would be terrible to be instrumental in returning them to that purgatory.* Laying his pencil on the sketch pad he turned to her with a nonchalant tone of voice. 'Where did they say the laboratory was?'

'Near Romsey, in Hampshire, the announcer said.'

'Well in that case it could hardly be these beagles could it. A long way east of here.' But, his brain racing, he pinpointed Romsey in his mind's eye. He was thinking that *the raiders with their absurd ideas of 'restoring domestic animals to nature,' could have driven west, to the far side of the estate or past it and dropped the dogs in some woodland, from which point they would perhaps instinctively have started roaming back towards the only home they knew.* then he said: 'Anyway, Mrs Harris, even if it turned out that it was these two that were stolen, I wouldn't want them returned to an animal experimentation place, would you?'

'No, I can't say as how I would. They do horrible things to them, don't they?'

'That's right. So let's forget about the radio report and this couple of mutts, shall we?'

'Oh, I won't breathe a word ... But, when you told me you might take all the dogs home with you, you said you thought you knew a good home for the lurcher. Where's that?'

'I hope a boy called Jerry Fuller's going to have him. You've been in these parts all your life. D'you know the name? Lives at Coneyhurst Corner.'

'Could be Madge and Fred Fuller's son. They're from Coneyhurst. They go to Bingo evenings in Tillston. Is he teenage, short, square shouldered, blue eyes, thick pale blonde hair swept back?'

'Exactly right.'

'Nice family that. How did he come your way then?'

'Well, I was walking the dogs along the public footpath close to here yesterday when this young chap approaching from the other direction suddenly took a close interest in Brill as I've named him. He called him 'Dusty' and started hugging him and patting him, and Brill seemed to know him. When I said his name was Brill, this Jerry Fuller insisted it was 'Dusty' and belonged to a couple called Sewell. I told him how I'd picked him up when Brill had got himself bumped into by a car and lamed.

'I then thanked the boy for telling me who the owners are, but when I asked if he'd be so good as to help me get Brill back to them he surprised me by saying "Oh no, please don't do that, they gave him a beastly life, chained him up tight all day and night". He said he lived in the same road and saw it all and had threatened the Sewells he'd go to the police about their treatment of the dog. I could see the boy really loved it. I said what a pity I couldn't offer Brill to him, but that was impossible him living next to the Sewells. At that his face brightened. He said he was getting his own pad any day now and could I wait. Then he gave me his name. It occurred to me that Tillston was a trifle too close for comfort to Coneyhurst. But I told him OK come and collect him, but make sure it's within the next three or four days as I'm leaving after that, and I brought him here to show him where he'd find Brill.'

'Well, well, Mr Clifford, I never thought you'd be parted from that lurcher. He reminds you of the one you lost doesn't he?'

'In looks yes, he's the split image, but he hasn't got Snakey's character. As I say I could see Jerry Fuller really adores him.'

'Oh well that takes care of that. But the labrador obviously belongs to someone. Nice looking dog,' said Mrs Harris. She scrutinised the beagles for a moment, bit her lip doubtfully, then returned her attention to his drawing. 'It's a really nice picture you're doing.'

'Thank you,' said Clifford, working with smudging touches on the highlights.

'I'll tell you what you ought to do a picture of, Mr Clifford.'

'Oh? What's that?'

'It's east of Ripley, over the river and up the top of the hill on Mr Harrington's land. It's a sort of Greek building, a temple so they say with stone figures surrounding it, women ..'

'What are they, muses, goddesses?'

'I wouldn't know what sort of women, would I. They might be, I suppose, and it's got a lovely ring of beeches round it. We had an artist staying at the manor two years back. He said he hadn't enjoyed making a picture of something more than that temple for a long time. You can see it from the footpath.'

'I know. I had a brief glimpse of it on my way here the week before last. It sounds fascinating. I might take you up on that.'

'You do that Mr Clifford, you won't regret it, I'm sure . . . Puffin's a little love, isn't he? There's no question of whose dog he is now, is there? Got a mind of his own, though. Always had.' When she leaned down to fondle the terrier's ear Puffin looked up at Clifford as if for reassurance that he should allow her to take such a liberty before submitting himself.

'He's great!', said Clifford, still intent on his sketch. And there's another thing there's no question of — who's top dog here. It's Puffin!'

'Yes, he'd be that, though he always set himself apart like from Mrs Bowes-Onslow's spaniels.' Mrs Harris glanced round the cabin. 'You've done wonders here with your carpentry. Mrs Bowes-Onslow will be pleased ... well I'd best be going now. I hope you like the fruit. The apples are Coxes' and the pears are really juicy.'

Clifford stood up now and faced her. 'I'm most grateful.'

'And don't forget to go drawing the Greek temple or whatever it is.'

'I won't, Mrs Harris, thank you for the advice.'

She turned to go, then paused and faced him again 'Have you met young Nigel and Sarah Harrington?'

'Can't say I have.'

'They only married about a month ago. Lovely wedding. Now they're living in Leawood Lodge, a cosy little cottage. Lovely young couple, they really are.'

'So the Reverend Richard told me.'

'Sarah's Mrs Bowes-Onslow's only daughter, but they don't always see eye to eye. I'm only reminded of it because she was up at the manor collecting guide books this morning. They're off to Normandy for the weekend. Spending three whole days there. She showed me the books she'd taken: *Wining and Dining in France* and *Europa Touring* and *Weekending on the Continent.*'

'They should be well away then.'

'Oh I do hope they enjoy themselves. Well, goodbye for the moment.'

'Au revoir, Mrs Harris.'

V

The silky auburn little dog showed the whites of his eyes, barked in frenzy and shrank from the storm. 'Don't be frightened,' Sarah Harrington spoke soothingly to it as the rain pattered on the window-panes of the Hostellerie du Chateau des Tourelles. 'It's only a shower.' She gave it her angelic smile, and, having been feeding it with pieces of her buttered *brioches* she now patted her lap, encouraging it to jump up.

Attention, madame! Le chien est sale, tres sale! The *patronne* emerged from behind the reception desk agitatedly, as fast as her expansive figure would allow and advanced on the table at which Nigel and Sarah were sitting. She repeated her warning in English. '*Madame*, please to be careful, the dog is dirty, eet 'as many flies. Or how you say — fleas? And your dress is so ... so *jolie*.'

Nigel agreed with the *patronne*. 'You'd better put it down, darling, it's probably got a disease, at any rate it'll dirty that lovely dress.'

'I don't mind, it's so adorable.' she replied, squeezing her husband's hand as the *patronne* waddled back to her desk with deep sighs. Sarah's fingers felt through the dog's fine golden coat to its ribs and leaned towards Nigel with a whisper. 'I don't think it gets a very good time here, it's thin as a rake ... But just look at those bent velvet ears and soft brown eyes,' she added, pressing its head towards him, 'don't they melt you?'

Gazing at her and ignoring the dog, Nigel cupped her face in his hands. 'Darling, I have to keep reminding myself how pretty you are.'

'Ooh yes, go on, go on, remind me!' And still stroking the little dog, Sarah craned her neck luxuriously as Nigel leaned across to kiss it. 'Oh, I still can't get over being Mrs Harrington. 'Mrs' and twenty last birthday. Pretty amazing. I think it suits me all the same.' Then she called across to the *patronne. 'Madame, encore deux brioches avec beurre, si'l vous plait, et café au lait.'*

'There's no need to show off, sweetheart,' Nigel teased, 'she speaks perfectly good English.'

The *patronne* registered his compliment. 'Yes, yes, I have many Americans here, many British, very popular with foreigners my hotel, I speak English many years. I bring you *brioches* and coffee. You are married short time, no?'

'Not long, this is our second honeymoon,' Nigel explained, *'notre lune de miel, comprends madame?* But very short. Only a weekend.'

'*Oui, monsieur,* that is charming. Ah, you Eenglish and your weekends of love! I make special arrangements for you, no? You lucky man, monsieur, you have a wife who ees *tres belle,* delicious.'

'*Lune de miel* indeed!' said Sarah giving Nigel's shoulder a playful slap. 'Who's showing off now?' The little dog, enjoying its position of privilege on her knees, coupled with the pieces of rich *brioche*, squealed sensually, wagged its disproportionately long and curly tail and put a tentative paw towards her face. Responding, Sarah planted a kiss on its muzzle and addressed the *patronne*. 'Er — madame, what is your dog called?'

'I call heem Coco. Hees breed is papillon, but not quite

pure, I think. Eet is not my dog. 'E come to beg food from my visitors and sometimes finds much food.' Illustrating what she meant, the *patronne* closed pudgy finger-tips on her mouth. 'And sometimes only leetle food. 'E does not get much this season, I think. Do not have heem near you, madame.'

'So he's a stray, poor little thing. Coco, Co-co,' Sarah repeated the name slowly. 'I'd like to take him home, he's so sweet. Would you mind, *madame,* if we took him away?'

Nigel grimaced and shook his finger at her as an indulgent father might. 'Oh really, darling, no way!...'

The *patronne* shrugged and made a face, too, but one of resignation as she approached their table waddling with short steps and another tray. 'You can take heem, madame, 'e belongs to no one, I do not want heem, 'e smell.' And, having lowered the tray, she put a finger to her nose and wrinkled her lips.

Sarah, undeterred by that gesture, sank her face into Coco's fur. 'M'm, yes, doggy, decidedly doggy. You're in dire need of a bath my little Coco. But I think you're quite adorable all the same. Nigel darling, let's take Coco home!'

'No way! You must be joking! Just imagine my father's face, my dad with his team of champion field-trial spaniels. Just think of his reaction if he'd discovered we'd brought in a dirty little mongrel from Normandy.'

'Yes, I can well imagine, pompous man that he is. Thank goodness you took after your mother. But it wouldn't be any of his rotten old business. Anyhow the *patronne* says it's a papillon ... and we wouldn't say we'd brought it over from here, we'd say it was a wedding prezzie.'

'Ha — some wedding present. You think of everything, you do, darling. And just to remind you, the *patronne* says it's not pure papillon, which makes it a mongrel. So, on those several different counts, let's forget it shall we?'

Their dialogue did not escape the *patronne*. 'I like you to have Coco, *monsieur, madame,* but I think you not get heem through the *douaine*, yes?'

'The customs!' said Nigel with a note of triumph. 'Exactly, *madame*, good point. Well of course there are no tariffs now, no import duty. But it's still illegal to take animals in from abroad ... So that counts the idea right out.'

Sarah, who had taken only one bite from her *brioche*, fed the remainder to Coco by carefully broken portions. 'See how ravenous he is!' She reverted to a hoarse whisper again. 'Oh, do let's smuggle him in, darling, let's finish our heavenly weekend with this adventure. Oh, please...'

'We'd have to register it and get an import licence. It'd have to go by special freight, then it would have to go into quarantine for six months.'

'Oh, phooey to quarantine. I don't want to lose him for six months. And I want the adventure of smuggling!'.

Nigel gave a dismissive laugh. 'I can just see the headline: *Merchant banker in court for illicit dog import*. Please get the notion right out of your beautiful head.'

'All that would add colour to the escapade. The whole thing would be too thrilling for words!'

'It would all end in disaster, I know it.'

'Nigel, you're in a funny mood. What's wrong, own up!'

'To tell the truth I'm dead worried about Zebedee. I'm afraid he must have been stolen.'

'I thought that was on your mind. But look at it this way, Coco could be Zebedee's replacement.'

'Oh marvellous idea, we'll put it into gundog training the moment we return,' he laughed with gentle sarcasm.

'It would be such an adventure to take Coco back,' said Sarah, her tone grown rather lame.

Nigel's laugh was tender. 'This jaunt has already been one of the best adventures of my life, entirely thanks to you, darling, it doesn't need embellishing ... Now look, it's stopped raining, let's go for a walk by the river before the sun goes down and take a look at that chateau we promised ourselves. We need to work up an appetite.'

When they stepped out, arms round one another's waists, Coco was close on Sarah's heels, looking up expectantly. After twenty minutes she insisted on stopping at a riverside café where she bought the hungry little dog a meat roll. 'There you are angel,' she told it, 'with the compliments of Auntie Sarah,' And to Nigel: 'Oh do be a sport, Nige. I've really set my heart on him.'

He laughed his half patronising, half indulgent laugh again. 'Oh, boo-hoo you've only one heart and I'd fondly hoped you'd set it on me.'

'Ninety-eight per cent of my heart is for passionate Nige, two per cent is for adorable Coco. As soon as we get back to the hotel I'm going to give him a lovely soapy smelly bath.'

'All right, darling,' said Nigel, with a wearily affectionate headshake, 'as long as you stop calling me "Nige".' With that he turned, lingeringly, to kiss her.

'I promise that, Nige darling,' she giggled as they drew apart. 'But one other thing ...'

'What's that?'

'How long do you think we'll be at Leawood Lodge?'

'I don't know, darling. Your problem's dad, isn't it, you don't like him?'

'Frankly no, he's so abrupt and scathing. It would be nice to put a bit more distance between him and us.'

'I'll keep him at bay, don't worry.'

'Oh thank you, Nige darling.'

The *patronne* organised a special honeymoon dinner for them. She made a pattern of pink roses on the tablecloth and lit pink candles and said 'I do all this special for you, Monsieur, Madame ... Monsieur is very fortunate man. We nevair have such beautiful young woman as Madame at the *hostellerie* before ...' They chose *terrine de foie de canard, leffeuillee de lotte poelees* and *croustillant au chocolat*, and they drank more wine than was good for either of them. The subject of Coco was not raised again until early next morning.

'I really am determined to take that little dog home with us,' said Sarah after a long pause as they lay in bed at six o'clock.

'God, how lovely you are!' was Nigel's reply, his hand on her breast, her head cradled between his neck and shoulder, his eyes searching the downy line of her arm.

'You're lovely, too.' As he tightened his embrace she returned his kisses fiercely, then she pulled away. You know I think fate decreed we should come here at this particular point in time and save that particular little dog.'

'You do, do you!'

She placed a forefinger on his nose, then planted a kiss very softly on his cheek. 'Darling, you said last night you'd never refuse me anything, remember? And I do so want to take Coco with us.'

'There'd be complications you know.'

'Not that we couldn't get over. I've really set my heart on him.'

'Have you indeed!'

'Now, darling Nige, we're not going to have the first row of our married life so early, are we?'

'Oh dear, I suppose your wish must be my command,' said Nigel, burying his face between her hair and neck again.

'Oh you're just divine, I'll pay the fine if we're caught.'

'You will indeed!'

'Oh Nige, you're brill!' And Sarah clasped him round

the neck with another long fervent kiss. 'I've got one of those tranquillizers left which the doctor gave me to settle me down before the wedding. I'll slip Coco half a one on the crossing ... Nigel, you're a great big angel! And another thing ...'

'Yes, darling?'

'Promise me you won't give another thought to Zebedee before we get back.'

'Well I must confess that he does worry me a lot.'

'You mustn't let it. I bet you a hundred pounds he's with your parents now, happy as a sandboy.'

To which Nigel's answer was a sigh and a headshake.

Three hours later when he went to settle his bill the *patronne* handed him the cardboard box, with ventilation holes cut round it, in which Coco was to be hidden for the landing at Portsmouth. Ten minutes after that the car was loaded, and the French waif, his silky golden coat shimmering like nuggets from the soapy bath Sarah had given him, was sitting on her knee looking excitedly through the windscreen.

The *patronne* chuckled with a vibration of her double chin at their departure. *Adieu monsieur, adieu madame ... adieu Co-co!*

Duly sedated, Coco remained very quiet on the crossing; Sarah behaved in a carefree manner; but Nigel showed his nervousness. He drank two double gins at the ferry bar which he would never normally have done. When they returned to the car he read a National Canine Defence League notice on the rear window of the one in front: 'A dog is for life, not just for Christmas'. And he winced. By the time the ferry doors opened Coco was secure in his box, over which they had loosely laid their overcoats and a rug.

'Now for the scary bit, the adrenalin bit,' said Sarah, biting her lip. 'O-oh, this is exciting!'

'The foolhardy bit you mean,' countered her husband. 'If you ask me, your Coco will probably be impounded and put down rather than having six months' quarantine. More than likely it'll be us that'll spend six months behind bars.'

But they steered unchallenged past the port authorities.

'There you are, easy as wink,' said Sarah as they drove from Portsmouth towards the Salisbury road and she leaned over to the back seat to release Coco. 'And there you are, good little sweetheart, quiet as a mouse weren't you then? Coming to life now are you? Clever Coco,' she crooned, lifting him onto her lap and smoothing down his silky fur.

The little cottage which is Leawood Lodge lies towards the road end of the drive leading to Leawood Hall. Nigel's mother, a slim, tall, white-haired woman in her mid-fifties, who had just turned on the heat for her son and daughter-inlaw, was there to greet them. 'Oh, you've brought a dog with you!' she exclaimed rather curtly after welcoming them with an embrace and a peck on the cheek as they got out of the car. 'Not from the Continent, obviously?' she added, arching her eyebrows.

'We picked him up from the Atkinsons on our way from Portsmouth,' Sarah invented. 'He's their wedding present to us, isn't he adorable?'

Nigel gave her a wry sidelong smile that went unnoticed by his mother.

What a funny little thing,' said Mrs Harrington senior, 'is it house trained?'

'Oh yes,' replied Sarah, 'he's wonderful in every way.'

'Funny to give a mongrel as a wedding present.'

'It's a papillon,' said Sarah proudly, 'a famous French breed.'

'That curly tail's too comical for words ... Well, there you are my dears, you're lumbered with it, aren't you, too rude to get rid of a wedding present, I mean ... Anyway I'm sure you'll be quite comfortable, I've turned on the central heating. Come and see us this evening, won't you ...'

Nigel and Sarah did that — though not, however, before Sarah had rather breathlessly telephoned a startled Angela Atkinson, making her party to the conspiracy but not mentioning that Coco had been smuggled from France. Coco greeted them deliriously on their return, but next morning he vanished. They thought he had been behaving rather strangely since his arrival at the lodge.

Nigel was standing at the bathroom window in his pyjamas, his face half covered in shaving lather, gazing across the garden to a point a hundred yards up the woodland ride beyond. He turned his head sharply towards the bedroom door. 'Darling, come quick and see what I see!'

Sarah left their bed indolently, rubbing her eyes and yawning. 'What's the trouble, lovey?' she asked.

'Well, look out there!' he pointed with a soapy razor.

She put her arm round his neck and peered through sleepy eyes. There, on the path, was the tiny golden figure of Coco, with a much larger dog, not facing it but going round in a mad circle and yapping, while the other stood quite still. 'Oh heavens above, Nige, how did he get out?'

'I let him out.'

'Oh, darling!'

'He has to relieve himself, doesn't he?'

'Yes, but surely only on a collar and lead until he's got used to his surroundings.'

'Well we haven't got a collar and lead yet, have we?'

'That's true, darling, but you ought to have watched him, he's a stranger in a strange land and I don't like the look of the other stranger.'

'Don't worry, I'll go down and fetch him in.'

'Golly, do be careful. The other one looks more like a wolf, horrible and spooky. It's put Coco into a right old frenzy.'

Nigel wiped his face, kissed his wife, slipped into some clothes and went outside. He was in no great hurry as he didn't really mind if Coco vanished, which the little dog had now appeared to have done — along with the big one. Nigel walked on down the path calling *Co-co! Co-co!* but only a couple of times and not very convincingly. Then he returned to the house feeling he had done his duty.

'So he's gone,' said Sarah, surprised at her husband's self consciously satisfied expression. She'd expected him to look crestfallen. 'Never mind, he'll be back quick enough when he's hungry — if that creepy one let's him.'

'He may not know the way,' replied Nigel hopefully.

'Of course he'll know the way, silly!'

By now Clifford had almost resigned himself to receiving new canine visitors every day. However, as he was past befriending newcomers, he couldn't be bothered to name Coco. This dog must be got rid of, along with the others and without delay. The French dog's arrival followed much the same pattern as the others. The summer-house inmates set up their familiar chorus that said 'Lupa's here again!' Clifford heaved a sigh, crossed to the verandah and glimpsed the longlegged, brown-grey bitch for a second before she turned tail on seeing him and loped off. And there, left alone, staring wildly and yapping at him was the little papillon cross-breed with the silky gold coat, sharp nose and long curly tail. Coco stopped barking and remained motionless, almost listless, as Clifford approached him.

Hello little fellow, you're a bit of a comic, aren't you, I suppose you are a little fellow under all that fur?... So thinking, Clifford lifted him up. Coco resented that and snapped at Clifford's wrist, but his teeth failed to make contact. *M'm vicious, skinny, too, but recently groomed by the look of it,* he conjectured. *I'll give it a bowl of food, but it needn't think it can stay here.* In fact, since Monica was due back the following day he'd hardened his heart and resolved to turn in the whole pack — except Puffin, of course, and Brill to the police first thing in the morning. *Yes I'll simply troop up to the Tillston police station and say 'There you are, I wish you luck in persuading one of the animal welfare societies to give them shelter.' Monica would, as Mrs Harris had warned, be horrified if she returned to find this lot here. But wouldn't she be delighted at the progress I've made in repairing and redecorating the cabin and clearing up the grounds. And then? Then I'll make my way back to Beachy Head with Puffin. Yet the thought of that lonely house still filled him with foreboding. The cabin was lonely, too, though I've really enjoyed myself there this past fortnight. Or was it nearer three weeks? The time had gone so quickly ... Meanwhile, I set myself one last mission. To make a watercolour painting of that Greek temple.* He looked anxiously at Coco. There was something rather disturbing about that little creature.

VI

Next day Clifford reaffirmed his decision to take up Mrs Harris's suggestion of having a go at making a watercolour of the Greek Temple. There was no question of having the pack along with him — except Puffin, of course — the Temple being on a neighbouring estate, and it would be irresponsible to leave this funny little silky-coated miniature, the latest arrival, at large. So, having fed Coco, he put him in the building with Regal, Seagull, Brill and Zebedee, who had all enjoyed a long dawn walk. He left the door semi-latched, so that if any of the larger ones were desperate they only had to give it a few hard knocks for it to spring open. Right now they seemed contented enough curled up together on his bed — except Coco, who withdrew into the furthest corner of the building where he shivered. Clifford's feelings about handing the unwanted dogs into the police were very mixed, to say the least. And how would the police themselves react to this 'invasion' of dogs. *I'd better telephone first,* he told himself, *to warn them I'm coming. That's to say if the telephone box hasn't been vandalised any more than it was already. But first the painting.*

'Come on, Puff!' he said, and armed with his folding artist's stool and his materials and with Puffin at heel, he set off eastwards down the public footpath. Crossing the stream onto the Leawood estate he climbed the two hundred yards which brought him level with the Temple. Walking the scarcely trodden track that linked the Temple with the footpath he spotted a gin trap set and baited between two stands of birch. Without hesitation he picked up a stick, pressed the platform, released the spring, pulled up the anchor and, with a gesture of disgust, threw the ugly contraption deep into a clump of brambles. He was, he knew, not so very far from the spot where Snakey ate the strychnine meat. Could this area be a veritable web of animal snares, pitfalls and poisons? Perhaps everything that he feared about the Leawood estate, coupled with all that Monica had implied, was really true? But he quickly put that out of his mind.

A few minutes later he was surveying the Temple from his selected range, seated on his canvas stool, sketch-pad on his knee, miniature fold-up watercolour box opened by his right foot, with Puffin in prone position, nose between forepaws, close on his left. He was rather pleased with his compact Winsor and Newton box with its metal hinged palettes folding over the tubes of paint, and its little brush and sponge and water bottle neatly incorporated, with the good variety of colours, all in the space of five inches by two by one.

The silhouettes of the gold-leafed beeches rose fluently and majestically against their grey-green trunks, making an elegant backcloth to the domed grey doric Temple with its long-robed goddess sentinels, one in front of each pillar. Between the grey of the trees and the stone edifice the sky shone cerulean and the forest floor sparkling bronze with early winter. Clifford, very contented with the scene, resolved that his composition would be no sketch but a fully fleshed painting, one that he would treasure for the memory of the place on his return to Beachy Head. When he began to draw he did so with total concentration.

Shortly after midday, as Clifford was endeavouring to give the goddesses a bit more paintbrush outline, Puffin suddenly got to his feet, hackles up, and barked urgently, the muscles of his powerful little neck bulging and taut.

'What is it Puff?' muttered Clifford abstractedly, a paintbrush in his hand as he washed in the shadow on the dome, another brush clenched between his teeth. Puffin's bark was reduced now to a low growl deep in the back of his throat. Above its monotone, in a moment, Clifford heard a rustle of leaves and a man's voice.

'And what, may I ask, are you doing here, mate?'

One brush still hovering over his delineation of the stone goddesses, Clifford, duly startled, removed the other from his mouth and looked up to see a thin, dark featured face with obstinate eyes under heavy eyelids and a deerstalker hat, a tall figure with a shotgun under his arm. 'Well, as you see — trying to make something of this old Temple. Lovely morning for painting.' Clifford returned his attention to the sketchpad.

'You're trespassing, this is private property, you'd better hop it quick.' There was as much menace in the man's tone as in his words.

'But I'm less than a hundred yards from the public footpath. Surely . . .'

'What the bloody hell they thought they were doing having that footpath public I don't know. Anyhow, it doesn't matter if you're right on the path, not with a dog running loose and disturbing my birds. It's not on a lead as it should be. So pick the little bastard up and clear off. Or I'll bring charges against you.'

Clifford began to get angry. He dipped his brush into the water container, rubbed it on the burnt sienna and poised above the painting again. 'Oh, to hell with your birds. I'm not in the habit of taking orders from rude people,' he said. 'Anyway, how do I know that you have the authority to order me off?'

'The name's Jarrow, I'm Mr Harrington's keeper and this is his estate you're taking liberties on.'

'Oh, are you indeed?' replied Clifford, getting up now and facing the man. 'Then I presume it's you who put down the gin trap which I set off and disposed of earlier this morning?'

'You *what*?' the keeper thundered, his grip tightening on his shotgun. 'What d'ye think you're doing interfering with private property?'

Clifford looked calm, but inside he was boiling. 'Gin traps are both cruel and illegal. I only did what any good citizen would have done. And I also have reason to believe you use strychnine and other poison for the purpose of killing the unfortunate creatures you believe are preying on your blasted pheasants . . .'

'What if I do? If I put down poison that's between Mr Harrington and me and booger all to do with you. Go on, get out of here!' Jarrow gave Jack's stool a sharp tap with his boot while Puffin, fairly bristling with fury, snapped at the keeper's ankles.

'I know the law. All poisons are illegal except certain anti-coagulants placed in hoppers for certain rodents. Anyway, I intend to finish my picture now,' said Clifford, resuming his seat. 'My dog's doing you no harm and nor am I. So I'll leave in my own good time ... Incidentally, I brought a dog of mine along here a fortnight ago. It was poisoned by a strychnine bait.' Clifford's heart was beating fast.

'If it was wandering round here it got what it deserved. And there's another I'm trying to get. A bitch that looks more like wolf than a dog. Been roaming our woods for weeks now. I wouldn't mind seeing that one screaming from my strychnine. Isn't yours by any chance is it?'

Clifford, in spite of himself, felt protective towards

Lupa. 'No ... and I've a good mind to report you to the police.'

'That'd get you nowhere. My boss is chairman of the magistrates' court. Now — clear off.'

Clifford was thinking *Christ this man killed Snakey and he thinks he can bully me.* He said: 'You tortured my dog to death and now you talk about trespassing.'

Jarrow seized him by the shoulder. 'Get moving, I said!'

Jack snatched the keeper's hand away, sat down again on his stool and deliberately resumed painting. Puffin was still yapping furiously at the man from a distance of ten feet. Jarrow walked back a couple of paces and held his twelve-bore at the ready, the knuckles of his right hand showing white where he clutched the small of the butt, thumb switching off the safety catch, forefinger across the trigger guard. 'Go on, you've got twenty seconds to get up to that path and away or I'll do your terrier in, which I've every right to do seeing it's where it don't belong.'

'If you so much as touch a hair of this dog's head I'll see you into prison for a good long stretch,' Clifford replied. But he knew the keeper meant business, was well aware the man would have no compunction about shooting any dog he found on the premises, whether accompanied by its owner or not.

'Well, are you going?' Jarrow's eyes blazed and a little muscle twitched on the corner of his downturned lip as he raised the butt of the gun into his shoulder and looked down the barrels at Puffin, who was yapping more feverishly than ever.

Normally, if Clifford had been accosted by an officious keeper he'd have simply picked up his things with a shrug and left. It was not only to save Puffin, but also the memory of Snakey, the memory of what this man had undoubtedly done to his lurcher, that prompted him to act as he did. It was a fatal moment. He made a sudden dash at Jarrow's gun and in the second that he lurched towards it, the keeper squeezed the trigger. The sound of the shot broke the stillness of the woodland like sudden thunder. Feeling a smarting sting, Clifford clutched his thigh. His face drained white as he dropped to his knees. When Clifford took his hand away from his thigh the keeper saw the blood on his fingers and panicked. 'You bloody idiot getting in the way of my gun!'

Mouth agape, he went as pale as his victim. 'Why couldn't you just do as you were bloody told, man?' But Jarrow was horrified at what he had done. '... Hurt bad, are you? Well, wait here till I get some help ... wait here man, d'ye understand?'

Clifford, head hung low with pain, did not answer. Nor did Jarrow, in his consternation, wait for a reply. Shouldering his gun he headed straight for the path that led to his Range Rover. What the keeper did not realise was that by the greatest good luck, the shot he had meant for Puffin, and which Clifford's interception deflected, had only torn the side of his trousers and sent no more than a couple of pellets into the outside of his thigh. The wound was not at all serious. What had brought Clifford to his knees was a slight anginal and heart attack. The real pain was not in his thigh but in his chest. Hearing the palpitations throbbing against his eardrums, he felt giddy and his breath came short and fast. He was clutching his chest. With 'Oh my god' on his lips Jarrow, thinking Clifford was responding to his leg wound, broke into a run, while Puffin barked furiously at his back.

Clifford took out the glyceril nitrate tablets prescribed by his doctor at home and which he always carried. He slipped one under his tongue. Then Puffin placed a tentative paw on his master's knee, inclining his tan-and-white head inquiringly. Clifford drew comfort from stroking the terrier's back vigorously until, after about ten minutes, his heartbeat returned to normal and the pain receded. But he still felt a little weak and shaky, and the moment he attempted to get to his feet the pain returned. He shifted the artist's stool, head still lowered.

A few minutes later he felt well again. At first he thought he'd go back to the cabin. Then he changed his mind. No, he'd let witnesses see what Jarrow had done to him, right here where it happened. Anyhow, he assumed that Jarrow, in his guilt, would have gone for medical help. And Clifford's wiser and more reflective self told him that he ought to get to a hospital for a check-up without delay.

The same current and cycle of thought kept rotating in his head in a wild, relentless vortex. *Would he recover sufficiently to walk back to Beachy Head or would he have to go by train? He'd had that anginal pain shortly after Kate died but he'd been given a sufficiently clean bill of health to start his journey across the Downs to this point within a month of that attack. He'd be all right this time, too, he was sure of it. In fact, he felt almost a hundred per cent again now. His thigh was smarting, but that's all. He'd much rather walk to Beachy Head — with little Puffin.* He smiled at the terrier, massaging the tan-and-white coat. The same doubts kept revolving in his brain. *Should he go into hospital? And in the meantime what would happen to those dogs at the cabin? He made the resolution he'd promised himself so often; he'd simply have to telephone the police and get them disposed of. With Monica due home tomorrow this was a matter of some urgency. Would she approve of all his repairs and redecoration of the cabin? And what about Puffin?* 'Oh you're a good boy, Puff, aren't you!'

His sudden exclamation sounded through the hush of the wood like someone in a church congregation speaking their thoughts when everyone else was in silent prayer.

'Yes, you're a very good faithful little dog. Worth all the others put together.' An hour went by and forty minutes more. And Puffin was his only comfort. Then the terrier jumped from Clifford's knees to stand on the leafmould, rigid, ears pricked again.

What was it? Clifford peered towards the point of Jarrow's departure again and sure enough, a few seconds later, there was the keeper with two ambulance men carrying a stretcher, trudging between the beeches towards him. Puffin snapped and snarled again at Jarrow, who stood back, shamefaced.

'How bad are you, mate?' asked the leading medical man.

'The gun shot's nothing,' replied Jack, still sitting in a hunched position. 'Trouble is I had quite a severe heart pain. I have a heart condition.'

'Crikey, we'd better get you into hospital sharpish. Think you can walk?'

'Good lord yes, I'm all right now. Really.'

'You need cardiac treatment, mate.'

'Perhaps you're right.'

'We can help you on the ambulance. We'll put you on our electrocardiogram.'

When they reached the point where the ambulance waited, Jarrow faced Clifford, looking guilty and very agitated. 'I'll be leaving now. It was just an accident, you understand? Gun went off without me knowing it.'

But Clifford was not in a kindly mood. This man had already murdered a dog of his and had been intent on murdering another. 'We'll see about that,' he replied, turning away grimly as Jarrow left, and climbing into the vehicle. Puffin, quick as a flash, was in beside him.

'You won't be allowed the dog, I'm afraid,' the ambulance man told him.

'Oh, surely - Puffin'll not be any trouble.'

'No dice, they're strict about that. D'you want to drop him in with a friend on the way or whatever?'

'No thank you. I believe he can look after himself.' Clifford surveyed Puffin with a rueful headshake, then climbed out of the ambulance, terrier under his arm and put him on the ground. He was absolutely confident that Puffin knew what was wanted of him. He trusted his good sense. Anyhow he was determined that he, Clifford, would be back at the cabin within the hour. 'Go on Puff, go home.' But Puffin only sat looking up at him whimpering uncomprehendingly.

When the ambulance set off in the direction of Tillston Cottage hospital Puffin sat, muscles taut, watching it move out of sight, still shivering a little and whining. Then, with flattened ears and drooped tail, but going straight as an arrow, he trotted, not to the cabin, but to Ripley Manor. There he barked continuously until, after about ten minutes, an astonished Mrs Harris answered his summons.

'Hello, Puffin, what's the trouble? Where's Mr Clifford?' She walked out onto the lawn and looked towards the perimeters of Ripley's extensive gardens. 'Mr Clifford?' she called. And called again. Then she turned to Puffin. 'What you doing here all by yourself then? Something up with him, is there?'

VII

Clifford objected strongly when they asked him to undress and go to bed after his consultation with the doctor. He insisted he was quite recovered. Indeed, a cardiac enzyme test verified there had been no serious heart attack. He was no sooner in that bed than he asked for a telephone. He rang the police and told the sergeant about his experience with Jarrow. The sergeant said he'd send an officer to the hospital to interview him. Clifford didn't mention the dogs — not at this stage. He began worrying about Puffin and, to a lesser degree, about the others. And his anxiety about completing his work on the cabin — the carpentry, joinery and decorating work — was never far from the surface of his thoughts either. Having taken so much trouble to make the building and its surrounds shipshape for Monica, in return for her hospitality, the last thing he wanted was for her to find the place infested with stray dogs. All the repairs and decoration to the cabin itself were as good as complete. But he had particularly wanted to fix the door of the little hut which backed onto the surrounding rhododendrons, and which served as a loo. It was hanging on one hinge, leaving the hut open to the elements. That was something that must be put right before he finally vacated the place.

He was getting in rather a panic, which he knew might

not be good for his heart; he was thinking impatiently, impulsively. *Puffin must be kept safe till I get out of here.* He tried to put through a call to Mrs Harris, but there was no reply. How the problems kept whirling about in his tired mind! *Those other pooches had to be got rid of, the sooner the better. There was only one thing for it now — come clean with the police.*

He telephoned again. 'Could I speak to the sergeant, please . . . Yes the Jack Russell terrier belongs to me and there's a lurcher to be collected by a young man of the name of Jerry Fuller. But the others are strays ... they're based in the cabin in the woods on the Ripley estate a little under a mile behind Tillston ... yes, that's where they've been fed, and, incidentally, it won't be long before they're starving. If you call on Mrs Harris, the housekeeper at Ripley Manor, and ask her to put food out for them ... yes, she'll show you the way ... you'll try to send along an RSPCA man as well? ... That's a very good idea. There's a dog warden in the village I believe? ...'

Mrs Harris was still wondering what had become of Clifford. With Puffin romping ahead she was walking to the cabin at the time he attempted to telephone her. She found no sign of life down there. Having admired Clifford's latest handiwork she stepped out onto the verandah, pondering, and leaving Puffin sniffing in all his old familiar corners. *Ah well,* she thought, *Mr Clifford's taken the other dogs for a walk and poor little Puffin got left behind by mistake. I know that Clifford often goes on very long walkies ...* She pressed her forefinger on her lower lip and frowned. *Or might Puffin have returned because the man was in some sort of trouble?* She regarded the terrier thoughtfully. And, as she did so something alerted him. Puffin cocked his tan ears, sprang down the verandah steps and stood rigidly, pointing his nose towards the rhododendron alleyway, the entrance to the compound. Then, with a look of intense interest written all over his little body, he trotted briskly out into the woodland. *Ah, that's good,* thought Mrs Harris, *the little blighter's heard Mr Clifford out there somewhere, I shouldn't wonder.*

Less than an hour after her return to Ripley Manor a policeman, accompanied by an RSPCA inspector, drew up on the forecourt in one of the Society's vans. 'Oh, that's dreadful!' she said when the constable informed her that Clifford was in hospital with a heart problem — having been shot in the thigh by the Leawood keeper. But she responded with her usual phlegm. 'Well I suppose you two gentlemen have come along to see about all those dogs of his? I expect you'd like a cup of tea first?'

'Thank you all the same,' said the RSPCA man, 'but we'd prefer to get straight on with the job.'

'What's happened to that horrible keeper?' Mrs Harris wanted to know.

'Mr Jarrow? His case won't be due before the magistrates till next week at the earliest.'

'I've just been down to the cabin,' she told them. 'That's where Mr Clifford was living with all those dogs, and I found it deserted. I took his own little terrier, Puffin, with me, but he's vanished now, too. You'd be on a wild goose chase looking for them now.'

'We'll just have to wait then,' replied the policeman, 'until we hear of sightings of them. Please keep us informed of any news that comes your way ...'

What sent Puffin's senses reeling that morning by the

cabin, the sound that alerted him but which did not register with Mrs Harris, was a repeat of Lupa's distant howling. As though it was a mandatory summons, an edict that was not to be disobeyed, as if he was an iron filing drawn to a magnet, he made a bee-line for the call. For, although he was by nature an independent dog, despite his attachment to Jack Clifford, he was also still strongly lured by her least sound, as well as by the sight and scent of her. Puffin had been top dog among the cabin canines, where really Clifford was overall top dog. But now he was absent the position was apparently assumed by Lupa. Puffin knew quite well that Clifford had not deliberately deserted him, he knew that his master was hurt and inadvertently detained. That is why his unerring instinct had told him to go to the manor and alert Mrs Harris. He was aware that he was otherwise powerless in the circumstances.

However, from the moment he heard Lupa's bidding howl, and turned away from Mrs Harris, everything else but that divine music was blocked off from his senses. When he reached Lupa deep in the forest, attracted as he was by her scent, he found her no longer howling but curled up with her muzzle resting in the fur of her wolfish tail and with an imperious self-satisfied look in her yellow eyes. Sitting around her, all gazing hypnotically at her brown-grey commanding body, were Brill, Zebedee, Regal and Seagull. Standing a little away from them, with staring eyes and gaping mouth, was Coco. Without hesitation, adopting his arrow-straight prone position, Puffin joined the circle. His every sinew, fibre, sense, like theirs, was concentrated upon her.

An hour later, scornful of them all, Lupa got up, yawned, stretched, licked her forepaws for a minute or so, then, with Coco always lagging behind, led her pack of male devotees back to the cabin. Having wasted no time in establishing that there was nothing to be had there, she pointed her muzzle towards the Brinkworth farmland beyond the woods. There, she was soon in pursuit of a myxomatosis rabbit. Unwittingly, it carried its white scut, as it ran, as an aiming mark for the bitch. Making a zig-zag course across the pasture, it left her behind at first; but, its eyelids swollen and closed up from the disease, it could not find a burrow, and Lupa snapped it across the back with her remorseless jaws as it tried to escape up a bank.

The other dogs crouched to watch her take a bite or two from its flank and leave the rest. Her male followers each sniffed the carcass but, finding her more interesting than the rabbit, returned their attention to Lupa. Then they all, except Coco — who only followed at a distance — began to hunt.

That evening Brill, snuffling up a hedgerow, came upon an unsuspecting leveret, and before it could get properly started from its form the greyhound-collie cross, fit and sharp as lightning from nearly a fortnight in Clifford's company, had it by the neck. There was much high-pitched squealing, kicking and struggling to be free by the juvenile hare, but Brill, exercising his strong sinewy neck and jaw muscles, held it fast, and with a final crunch of his dagger-like canine teeth on its skull, sent it limp.

He pulled the warm body into the open, began tearing its fur and tasting its rich blood and, being very hungry, whined with delight. He had just ripped away a first mouthful of flesh, however, when he felt Lupa's menacing presence close at hand. He stopped eating and turned to her with a snarl, eyes blazing. Lupa's lips curled showing the yellow of her fangs. She placed a foot on the dead animal's shoulder. Brill snapped at her, at which she hurled herself at him, goring him deeply on the flank.

The others, rivetted by the challenge, were agog as they

watched the combatants roll over and over on the turf in desperate battle for some five minutes, until at last a vanquished Brill slunk away, head hung low, an abject expression on his jowl and in his eye, tail between his buttocks, craven, diminished in every aspect. Lupa, the dictatrix, *la belle dame sans merci,* returned to take the leveret while Brill nursed his wounds with little cries of pain. But for one who was appreciably lighter and weaker and less aggressive by nature, he had put up a most creditable fight. The other dogs gave signals — signals that would not have been visible to human eye — acknowledging his courage.

Regal, Seagull and Zebedee approached Lupa in a slavishly solicitous manner, encircling her like worshippers at the shrine of some avaricious deity, while Puffin, waiting to see if she might leave a morsel of the carcass, surveyed the scene with a quizzical look, and Coco still kept his distance. Brill sat up now, brow puckered, ears cocked, head on one side, apparently accepting Lupa's principle that she had first claim on everything that was caught. So far Lupa had had little difficulty in retaining her leading position in the power struggle. But Puffin, although still in awe of her, was no longer party to the general homage. He was, as he was about to demonstrate, beginning to assert his naturally independent character.

The dogs spent the night in a spinney of beeches and, at dawn Puffin, hearing a soft rustle of leaves a few yards away, stood up abruptly. It was a squirrel. He gave chase and had his teeth into it just as it reached a beech tree's green bole. With his terrier tenacity he gripped it, and shook and shook and shook until the life ebbed from the bushy-tailed rodent. All the others were immediately up and about. Puffin took no notice of them. Famished as he was, he bit hard into the squirrel's pelt. But no sooner had he begun tucking into the nutty flesh than Lupa trotted up, showing her fangs and demanding that first refusal which she had not so far failed to claim. Puffin stopped eating for a moment and, with a proprietary paw on the grey hide, he gave the bitch a long low growl from the depths of his throat, He was telling her, in effect, that this was essentially his kill and that he would not, despite his inferior size, let it go without a fight to the death. And, gradually, she got the message.

He turned from her to the squirrel again and resumed his meal. Lupa was at first disdainful of such an apparently insignificant challenger. She drew closer, giving a terrifying ululating whine that ended in hideous barking. Puffin stood his ground, switching his attention with a continuous growl and stiff turns and flicks of his head from his kill to her and back again, then continuing to eat while he snarled more fiercely, body tensed, with signals that told Lupa he had no intention of relinquishing his prize. Placing her elbows on the ground, raising her backside in the air in a menacing posture and bringing her yellow eyes close to Puffin's eyes, the lupine bitch began a fresh, hectic snarling and yapping.

Then, when she snatched at the squirrel's tail, Puffin sprang at her head and with his needle-sharp teeth bit her on the lip as he had once done at the cabin, drawing blood. She squealed, then went for the dead animal again. But Puffin would not yield and, with every second that passed, his exceptional terrier willpower prevailed. Perhaps he was aware that, with a quick dozen bites, she was quite capable of dispatching him, but he also seemed to sense quite strongly that if he remained firm he would win. And that was his triumph.

It was as though the spell which Lupa had cast on him was broken, temporarily at least, by this incident of the squirrel. Her hackles subsided, she drew her tongue nervously over her whiskers, pressed her ears onto the back of her head and, with a drooping posture, slunk to one side. For she knew she could not let this little terrier get away with his victory and still retain her supreme position in the pack. Nonchalantly, she started licking between the toes of a forefoot as though she had never been interested in the squirrel in the first place. But Brill, Zebedee and the beagles, seeing her so easily defeated by one so small, now almost scorned her and regarded Puffin with a new admiration and respect. In those few minutes he had reclaimed for himself the station of top dog, the position he had held, unchallenged, at the cabin. Now, unhindered, and basking in this fresh glory, he consumed what he needed of the squirrel, this being his first experience of the flavour, and he left those parts of it which he disdained to the others.

And yet, and yet ... although he was no longer dominated by Lupa, she still held a compulsive fascination for him. Now subservient, she followed him. Later in the afternoon he led the way towards the east side of Tillston. And there a melodrama occurred to change all their lives.

VIII

Nigel was now quite sure which of the two losses caused him the most anxiety. Up to the time of his and Sarah's return from France the desertion of his black labrador, Zebedee, his beloved young gundog, had been his only concern. But now that Sarah was kicking up such a fuss about missing the wretched little Coco — and he himself was worried stiff their crime would be discovered — if he was obliged to choose between the recovery of Zebedee and that of Coco he'd certainly opt for the latter. Yes, the miniature French pooch had definitely taken top place on his agenda. Anything to keep Sarah happy. Besides, just supposing Coco was handed into the police or a dog warden or whatever and enquiries led to them discovering that the brute had been smuggled in over the Channel? The prospect of being exposed was too awful to contemplate. Nor was this just an ethical issue, linked with keeping on the right side of the law. There was also a question of pride, of pride in their local reputation, the honour of the family name and the Leawood estate.

Nigel felt so guilty about having given in to Sarah and shared in her conspiracy that he felt the need to confide in someone about the problem. *There was only one possible candidate as confidante,* he was thinking, *my mother-in-law. The more I consider it the more I'm convinced. Monica has a name for sorting out other people's dramas and picking up the bits; she's someone to be trusted with a secret; and she'd do anything for Sarah. She must be just about back from Scotland by now. Yes, that's it, I'll give Monica a ring — without letting on to Sarah, who'll almost certainly make a song and dance about it.*

Even as these musings circled in Nigel's head Monica was proceeding up the Ripley drive, home from her Highland holiday.

Hearing the taxi crunch on the gravel just as the sun was sinking towards the skyline, Mrs Harris ambled out to welcome her employer back and help her with her luggage.

'Hello, you're looking well,' said Monica cheerfully, 'how's everything been going here?'

'Fine here at the manor, but that Mr Clifford, who was in the cabin, he's got himself taken into hospital — Tillston General,' Mrs Harris replied.

'Oh, poor man, nothing gruesome, I hope? Let's go through to the library and talk about it,' said Monica, taking off her coat.

'Yes ... Well it is quite bad. He got shot in the leg by Jarrow, the Leawood keeper.'

'Oh, my God! ...' Monica looked up sharply.

'Well that was only quite slight, luckily. Jarrow was really trying to shoot little Puffin as I understand it. Mr Clifford had a touch of heart trouble. That's what he's in for.'

Monica sat upright, a hand clutching the arm of the library sofa. 'You're not *serious!*'

Mrs Harris continued explaining in her placid manner. 'I'm afraid I am that. And another thing, they've taken a statement from Mr Clifford. Jarrow's been charged with assault and malicious wounding and remanded in custody.'

'Heavens above! Any reaction from Mr Harrington?'

'Well, they do say he's hopping mad, because he's chairman of the magistrates' court, but he won't be allowed to hear Jarrow's case, of course, him being an employee. I understand Mr Clifford's also brought charges against Mr Jarrow for using illegal traps and poisons.'

'Bully for Mr Clifford. I must pay him a visit. Is Puffin with us now?'

'Well, it's a mystery about Puffin. He turned up on the back doorstep here after Mr Clifford's calamity, me not knowing about that just then, and I took the little fellow, Puffin that is, down to the cabin, and while I was looking round Mr Clifford's handiwork — he's done a wonderful job there I have to admit — Puffin shot off into the woods and I haven't seen him since.'

'Doubtless he'll be back here when he's hungry.'

'I've left some food down there for him, too. But Puffin's not the only problem.'

'O-oh?' Monica arched her eyebrows. 'Something to do with brother Richard?'

'No, he's all right. Upstairs in his room where he's usually to be found. No — I have to tell you that quite a number of stray dogs occupied the cabin during your absence.'

'Strays? How's that?'

'Mr Clifford seemed to collect them, not purposely mind, they just turned up. It seems there's been a big female dog, German shepherd type, rather nasty I understand, and — well, in an interesting condition, as they say — which has been attracting them in.'

'Dear oh dear, and meanwhile they're roaming the estate I suppose, making a nuisance of themselves?'

'Well, there have been one or two complaints locally.

He's a funny one that Jack Clifford. I can't make him

out. Anyhow, he's that worried he phoned the police, and a sergeant I think it was came here along with a chap from the RSPCA. I showed them the cabin and they're making plans to have the dogs rounded up.'

'M'm — I hope they succeed very quickly. A stray pack could get up to all sorts of mischief. I'll go and see Mr Clifford first thing in . . .' Monica was cut short by the telephone. Mrs Harris took the call. 'It's Nigel Harrington for you.' She handed Monica the receiver.

'Nigel? . . . M'm, I got back half an hour ago . . . Yes, I remember Zebedee, nice young labrador. No, so far as I know he hasn't turned up here. Ran away during a shoot, how extraordinary . . . And you've lost another one, how careless of you! This would appear to be the great lost dog period in the Ripley history . . . Well yes, we seem to have a similar problem here to tell the truth . . . No not my spaniels, perhaps they're the only ones with halos round their little heads these days. But Mrs Harris tells me our cabin resident, Jack Clifford, has proved quite a magnet for stray dogs. So perhaps Zebedee's there . . . No you won't find him now, Clifford's in hospital and his pack's on the loose . . . Anyhow, tell me about your other one . . . M'm, so Sarah insisted on bringing it back. Have you got no control over the girl at all! How about quarantine?. . . Oh she did, did she? Trust her to do something really silly . . . Well you're to blame, too, really aren't you, Nigel? . . . I know, I know, she can be very persuasive . . . No, of course I won't tell your parents, provided you do your utmost to find the little blighter. It could get you into all sorts of trouble . . . Don't worry, old Monica will combine the roles of delphic oracle and fairy godmother. Sarah's put her foot in it often enough and she'll do it again . . . Yes, relax, we'll keep quiet about it for the moment. But I think you'd better come up and pay me a visit, don't you? . . . .

No, don't bring Sarah with you this time.'

Replacing the receiver, she thought *no — no I won't try and fit in that visit to Jack Clifford. Too many problems to cope with here. But poor man . . .*

'Something else the matter?' asked Mrs Harris.

'Nothing that can't be handled quite easily,' replied Monica sounding more optimistic than she felt.

Just about the time of those conversations the dogs, led by Puffin, and all hoping to find scraps, scavenged briefly and very tentatively around the dustbins of one of Tillston's outlying housing estates. Then they made for the stand of birches flanking the children's playground, which was adjacent to the public car park. The half-dozen kids who had been gallivanting there had now drifted away, leaving just one girl of about twelve, who was still enjoying herself on a swing while chewing on a bar of chocolate. That girl was Candy Sewell. The swings were just in sight of Candy's mother who was waiting in her car. While Puffin, Lupa and Zebedee remained resting in the birches, Brill and the beagles, with Coco staggering behind, began sniffing across the playground. As they approached Candy, the child stopped swinging as though she'd seen a ghost. She ran towards the car park. 'Mum, mum, come here quick!'

'What is it, Candy?'

'Dusty's here, mum!'

Sharon Sewell got out of the car and started towards the swings. 'Where'd you see it, love?'

'There — there! With them two beagles and the little tiny one.'

Frightened by the commotion Brill, Regal and Seagull stopped hesitantly in their tracks, ears pricked in alarm, before withdrawing to the birches, leaving only Coco yapping at mother and daughter.

Mrs Sewell looked dubious. It was getting dark and visibility was poor. 'I don't think it *was* him, Candy.'

'I'm sure it was, mum. It was his markings exactly.'

'Well, no one could see a dog properly in this light. And anyway it's much too late. You're not having any more than five minutes on that swing, d'you hear?' Sharon Sewell turned back to her car.

'Oh, 'oright mum,' said Candy sulkily, and took another bite from her chocolate bar. With a carefree skipping run she dashed to the swing, pushed hard against the ground, heaved with her body and,was soon flying high.

Something about the rush of the swing and Candy's kicking legs put Coco in a frenzy. Now directly underneath the swing he was not only yapping but attempting to bite Candy each time the seat swung downwards. Candy let out a vicious kick, missing Coco's head by inches. In the effort of doing this she dropped her bar of chocolate. Determined to retrieve it and confident that such a minute dog could do her no harm, she stepped down from the swing and stooped to pick up the remains of her precious bar. With Candy's face only a foot or so from the ground, Coco jumped up and bit her very hard on the cheek, then snapped up the chocolate and made a giddy sprint for the birches. Candy, bleeding profusely and holding her face with both hands, went screaming to her mother, who climbed out of the car, arms outstretched.

'For heaven's sake, what's happened now, love?'

'Horrible little dog bit me, one of them with Dusty, that's what,' she screamed.

'More blood than damage, dear, by the look of you. Take your hands away, let's have a proper decko,' ordered

Sharon Sewell, picking a handkerchief from her handbag and wiping her daughter's cheek. 'M'm, quite nasty though. I daresay you could pick up something dangerous from a dog bite. I'm taking you straight round to the surgery. And just get the idea of the other one being Dusty right out of your head. Forget about Dusty, see?'

The incisions on Candy's face worried the doctor, too, especially when Candy told him that the little dog had been turning wildly in small circles, snapping. Having taken the precaution of an anti-tetanus jab he telephoned the hospital and booked her in within the hour. Despite reductions in the hospital staff Candy was seen straight away. It was Candy's description of Coco's behaviour more than the wound itself that worried the house doctor. He tested Candy for rabid antibodies. Her wound was washed very thoroughly with disinfectant, and the doctor also gave her a jab of the appropriate vaccine. The police were informed that the hospital had a possible case of rabies on their hands and, next morning, the head of the relevant branch of the district council was told.

Candy cried through most of the night, in terror rather than pain. During her snatches of sleep her nightmares were more of Brill or, as she saw him, Dusty, than of Coco, and when the nurse came to take her temperature in the morning, halfway between sleep and wakefulness she was shouting 'Dusty — go away you horrible thing!' She pleaded to be allowed to go home, but was told that she must remain in hospital for the time being. Meanwhile a swab confirmed that she had received a rabies bite.

That night Brill, Regal, Seagull, Zebedee, Lupa and Puffin slept peacefully in Pheasant copse, not far from the very spot where Clifford had started his painting of the Temple. For it was Puffin who led them. Coco, who was still there with them, but a few yards from the group, did not rest at all. He picked a quarrel with Regal and Seagull, both of whom had become much more self-assertive and aggressive in their wild state. After a short struggle, given their combined ferocity and superior weight, they killed Coco, but not before he had bitten each of them deeply with his tiny needle-sharp teeth. By dawn both beagles lay dead, too.

IX

There had been no serious signs of rabies in the British Isles, outside quarantine, since as long ago as 1969, and the local authorities, determined to take no chances, acted with due vigour and resolution, in implementing their contingency plans. One or two people had contacted the police saying they thought they'd had glimpses of the dogs roaming in a small pack on the outskirts of Coneyhurst and Tillston, as well as in parts of the Ripley, Leawood and Brinkworth estates. All those areas and the adjacent fields were marked on the maps as being within the zone under suspicion. The Ministry of Agriculture warned local landowners and farmers in and around the 'affected area' to take due precautions with regard to their livestock; the masters of the local hunt were requested to hold their hounds in kennels until further notice; pet owners were instructed to keep their animals shut up or, if letting them out, to ensure they were muzzled and leashed.

In the old days the procedure was to sweep through the infected area with guns, shooting all mammals on sight. That course of action, while dispersing any wild life, failed to treat the problem of potentially rabid foxes which, being prone to bite one another in pursuit of their territorial claims, would be the chief spreaders of the disease. With the advent of the effective vaccine, the contingency plan included (as it does to this day) two principal tactics: to ring the vicinity concerned with vaccine bait, in order to immunise the foxes and to round up any domestic animals, still at large. The only evidence about the Tillston outbreak so far was from the swab taken from Candy Sewell and her description of Coco. The Ministry had already sent out its edict, and the local authority, along with the police, were preparing their tactical plan. Meanwhile, there were others with their own ideas as to how the problem should be solved.

'You're looking black as hell, Bob,' and with good reason I shouldn't wonder, said Ted Sewell, putting his glass of beer on the pub's corner table where glum-faced Bob Hood sat staring. Sewell settled his heavy frame next to his Coneyhurst neighbour and took a swig of beer. 'I saw that *Gazette* report this morning 'bout them dogs killing your sheep, rotten bastards.'

Hood looked up briefly, unsmilingly. 'Yeah, seven killed by the buggers and ten more so badly mauled I had to destroy 'em. Diabolical I call it.' He regarded Sewell more closely. 'And what about you, Ted, you've got even more reason than me for hating bloody dogs since that little bugger gave your Candy a rabies bite . . .'

Young Artie Crawford, a building worker, sitting at the next table with his newspaper spread across it and his sandwich lunch next to his shandy, began to take a close interest in this conversation, but his eyes never wavered from the newsprint. Tillston's Red Lion was crowded, but Artie wasn't missing a word of the adjacent dialogue.

'Hate'em?' spluttered Sewell. 'That ain't strong enough

for the way I feel. I'd like to see every bloody pooch in the world dyin' a miserable slow death. I had one up to coupla weeks ago, lurcher we called Dusty, a load o' trouble and expense he was, no use to anyone. Wife had the bright idea of taking him for a walk and went and lost 'im. Good riddance. Wouldn't be surprised if he isn't one of your sheep killers. They're dirty devils the lot of 'em, a right menace.'

''Cept them as does a good job of work for their living like my two sheepdogs . . .' Course, twenty or thirty years ago they'd have had the guns out after a rabies case and done 'em all in, all that's loose and out in the open. But you hear what they're goin' to do now? Catch 'em up and give 'em a nice cosy home in an animal shelter — yeah, them as got my sheep.'

Sewell shook his heavy head slowly from side to side in sympathy and lit another cigarette. 'Ay, and them that's claimed'll likely go stray again and have another go at your flock. Bloody ridiculous, I . . .'

'That idiot keeper of old Harrington's,' Hood interrupted; 'thinks 'e's so bloody marvellous at keepin' down predators, but this lot of dogs gave Jarrow the slip every time.'

'Now he's on bail awaiting trial for shooting some artist bloke,' added Sewell ruefully, 'that'll larn 'im.'

'M'm, he claimed to destroy a lot of foxes did Jarrow, but he didn't stop 'em going after my lambs every spring . . . You know what the so-called authorities've got in mind for the foxes, Ted? Feed the little darlings on anti-rabies vaccine. Wonderful ain't it. Keep 'em healthy.' Hood gave a laugh, thick with irony.

'Bloody brilliant. But, about them dogs, Bob, you know the one I'd like to tear limb from limb, don't you, the little bugger that bit Candy. My Candy loves them swings in the playground. You should see the look on her little face when she's swinging really high. A right picture, a picture of happiness. Then somebody's rotten dirty little dog goes 'n spoils it all for her.'

'I bet you'd like to get your hands on that one but if it was rabid, which it must have been, it'd be dead as a dodo by now. Or maybe it was just a carrier ... I got a favourite, too — terror of a German shepherd, Alsatian type, that's been loose and wild around the countryside living on its wits for months. And if I don't do something about it in double quick time we'll have the Council men, police, dog wardens, RSPCA, you name it, putting a tranquilliser dart in it. Then we'll have some fool claiming it and before we know where we are it'll be the terror of the whole countryside again.'

'What've you got in mind then, Bob?' enquired Sewell, draining his glass.

'Now if you keep dead quiet about this, I'll tell you. Me and my two boys are going out with guns and we're going to get that brute along with any other dogs we come across . . .'

At this Artie Crawford leaned a little closer, straining to catch every word, though still appearing to be busy reading and munching sandwiches. He had a close friend with a dog somewhere out there. That friend would be very interested in Bob Hood's intentions.

Sewell, like Hood, lowered his voice. 'You'll need to be quick about it, Bob, Council people'll be out soon.'

'Not before dawn tomorrer they won't.'

'M'm, I've got a 12-bore, mind if I join you?'

Hood glanced towards Artie Crawford before facing Sewell again. 'Done much shooting?'

Sewell smirked slyly. 'I just about know one end from t'other.'

'All right, you come too, we could do with an extra gun,' he whispered. 'But for Gawd's sake keep your voice down now, we don't want the whole bloody neighbourhood knowing about it.'

'Where'll we meet?'

Hood gave Artie Crawford another suspicious look. Then he said 'my boys have been doing a bit of tracking. Dogs were up in Pheasant Copse last evening and they reckon the Alsatian's howling came from there through the night. Meet us six o'clock on the road at the Avonlea bridge, right?'

'Right.'

'You know where my tenancy is, between Pheasant Copse and the old Roman road. Well, we'll spread out and come up behind . . . We'll need to be quiet as mice mind. That big dog's about as artful as they come.'

'All right, Bob, we could be having a spot o' fun, eh? See you in the morning mate . . .'

This was the gist of what Artie Crawford heard. When the two conspirators left the Red Lion he finished his shandy, folded his newspaper and, thoughtfully, pedalled back to work, back to the building site on the west side of the village. And the first thing he did when he got there was to relate his eavesdropping experience to the close friend who had an interest in this particular situation — Jerry Fuller.

Jerry was not only aware of Candy Sewell's fate, of Clifford's incarceration in the same hospital and of the charge against Jarrow but he'd also kept himself informed about the Council's plans for dealing with the rabies emergency. So far as he was concerned Brill, alias Dusty, had been promised by Clifford and was now his property. Up to now he'd been content in the knowledge that, if the Council people caught up with the dog, it would be safe and he'd simply claim it. But Artie's intelligence from the Red Lion put a quite different complexion on things. If Sewell and Hood located the dogs that had been hanging around Jack Clifford — and it sounded as if they'd have every chance of doing so — they'd bung them full of lead first thing in the morning. Jerry, coming from Coneyhurst, knew Hood's reputation as well as Sewell's: a hard, bitter, unyielding man. So he acted fast. He told his foreman he was feeling lousy and took the afternoon off. Then he collected a collar and lead and a few biscuits for enticement, got on his motor bike and headed for the Avonlea bridge. He started walking on precisely the same route related to him by Artie from Hood's description in the pub.

Once on the rides in Pheasant Copse he started calling 'Dusty! Dusty!' Then he remembered Clifford's name for the lurcher and called 'Brill! ... Brill!' whistling in between the name. It was not long before he found his first evidence, quite sensational evidence. Lying on the leafmould, about a hundred yards from the Temple, he came across the tricolour bodies of the two beagles, Regal and Seagull, both dead, mouths open, eyes staring crazily. On close examination he found the tiny teeth-marks of Coco's bites, oozing blood, and guessed at once that they were rabid. He was sorry for them. They must, he reckoned, have died a miserable and traumatic death. He was pretty sure that pair hadn't been with Clifford when he'd met him last week on the Ripley estate. Maybe they'd joined Clifford's pack later? Leaving the beagles, Jerry searched all round Rockingham Copse, back through Pheasant, then all round Hazels and back to Rockingham again. And there an extraordinary sight confronted him as he came between the trees towards a broad track leading to Leawood. He quickly concealed himself behind an oak trunk.

Sixty yards or so away a young woman walked slowly from left to right across his path, holding a small dog with its head hanging limp. Jerry noted that she wore jeans, a Barbour coat and headscarf, a pretty girl but sad looking. He saw that she was crying. The little dog she carried was a bright russet colour, very silky, with a white stripe leading from its nose, broadening as it passed between the eyes to the top of the head. Jerry could just see part of its curly, bushy tail flopping below the girl's other hand. Dead — no doubt about that. And nothing, he thought, could have answered the police description of the rabies suspect more closely. But he'd keep quiet about that, seeing that he was up here in the no-go area. The less said the better. He panicked briefly with the thought that Brill might have received a rabies bite.

The minute the girl was out of sight he stepped onto the path and began walking quietly in the opposite direction. He checked his watch anxiously. He'd been out there well over an hour. *Ah well,* he thought, *if Brill's not up here chances are Hood and Sewell won't find him either.*

In the very moment that Jerry harboured this hope a small tan-and-white terrier moving with all the frenzy of a wound-up clockwork toy, crossed his path. Next, a large grey-brown dog came out of the wood onto the track and looked at him for a second with yellow malevolent eyes. Giving a deep groan of alarm and flattening its ears, it then sprang into the seclusion of the opposite side and was quickly out of sight. Hard on its heels, a little further down the path galloped a labrador.

And right behind that came the one Jerry was looking for. Brill the lurcher, tousled and muddy-looking, white, gold and black, stood dead in his tracks, staring wonderingly at Jerry, who called softly to him 'Brill, come on old boy!' And Brill almost certainly identifying this as a friendly voice from the past approached him with a tentative wave of the tail. Still suspicious, the lurcher came closer, paw by paw, and sniffed. Yes, the young man's odour too, was familiar, so now the tail wagged briskly, swinging Brill's body with it. He licked Jerry's hand.

Well old friend, you haven't half been in the wars since I last clapped eyes on you, went Jerry's unspoken thought seeing the shabby mud-spattered coat and the wounds inflicted by Lupa the previous day. He hugged and patted the delighted lurcher. *Anyhow you're mine now and you won't be called Dusty no more that being what the Sewells called you. I'll stick to Mr Clifford's name, Brill. Oh it's good to see you again, Brill!* Jerry gave his dog the biscuits he had brought, and Brill consumed them whole. Then he buckled on the collar, and soon finding the ride that would lead him to his car he walked briskly along it, whistling with satisfaction at his luck in finding his dog at last. Whistling, too, because it was a lovely evening and the trees were enveloped in a golden haze from the November sunset.

He wondered about the young woman. That little dog of hers had more than likely died of rabies after biting the Sewell child. *It certainly tallied with the details of the one reported to the police. Perhaps, perhaps he should ... No? Well no, he wouldn't report that woman and her little dog to the police. He might start something he'd regret.* After another five minutes' walk, he cursed inwardly at seeing a stout middle-aged man, with fury on his florid face and a walking stick in his hand, coming towards him and moving more determinedly as he approached. Although Jerry didn't want to be spotted up there by anyone it was too late to dodge out of the way.

'What the hell do you think you're doing here?' the man roared.

Jerry had no idea who this stranger was. 'I might ask you the same thing,' he said impassively. As he had demonstrated with the Sewells, Jerry was no respecter of persons, and he knew this to be in the council no-go area.

The man struck the ground violently, two or three times, with his stick and flew into a rage. 'The name's Harrington and I happen to own these woods!'

Jerry, though now feeling rather uneasy, continued to appear calm. He had this facility for adopting a carefree air in tricky situations. 'I was only collecting my dog. There's been a case of rabies you know, and there's to be a lot of action here tomorrow, so they say.'

'Of course I bloody well know, you insolent young devil,' shouted Harrington. 'Didn't you hear? I own the place. My keeper's gone and I'm up here seeing where my pheasants are before they start their nonsense tomorrow ...' He looked at Brill. 'I wouldn't be surprised if that mongrel of yours isn't rabid, it looks motheaten enough. Now clear out of here, will you, before I have you up for trespass!'

So that's who this is! Jerry, who took exception to being addressed in this aggressive manner, was now bent on irritating the landowner further. He flicked back his hair with a cheeky smile. 'I know your keeper's gone. Been remanded for trial, hasn't he? Been a bad boy. It's all the buzz round these parts. But that's no good reason for you losing your cool with me.'

Harrington was now verging on the apoplectic. 'You get yourself and your dog off my property at the double or you'll have a hiding you won't forget!'

To Jerry's horror Harrington raised his stick as if to strike Brill who, having experienced the darker moods of the human race all too often before, shrank away barking, hackles raised. Instinctively dropping Brill's lead, Jerry flew at Harrington, grabbed the stick, wrenched it from his hand and pushed him very hard into the ditch running adjacent to the ride, a ditch filled with muddy water from the autumn rains.

'How dare you attack me!' spluttered Nigel's father,

sitting on his backside in the water.

'Well, you were going to hit my dog, weren't you?' replied Jerry, flinging the walking-stick into the ditch. 'He was doing no damage.'

'You'll hear a great deal more about this. I happen to be chairman of the magistrates' court, apart from being the landowner here,' countered Harrington, trying to heave himself from the water.

Jerry picked up Brill's lead. 'If anyone hears more about it it'll be you, and you'll be lucky if you don't follow your keeper to jug, assaulting an innocent dog like that . . . Do you know who I am?' he added as an afterthought.

'I shall make it my business to find out,' promised the wet, prostrate figure, attempting to extricate himself from the mud.

Come on Brill, he whistled. *Perhaps it's just as well he don't know who we are,* thought Jerry, as he continued towards his motor bike. While he walked (at a much faster pace than when he started) he found himself wondering again who *that classy young woman with the little dead dog might be.* He would have been astonished to learn that she was the daughter-in-law of Edwin Harrington and the daughter of the owner of the neighbouring Ripley estate. He was pretty sure old Harrington wouldn't say anything. After all, he'd no business being out, even on his own estate, while the Council embargo was on. What next? Jerry asked himself. He shuddered at the thought of those three other stray dogs he'd seen up there in the woods being gunned down by Sewell and Hood. Especially that perky little terrier which he remembered as being Jack Clifford's pride and joy. If he told the police he'd more than likely be prosecuted for not declaring Brill, or for being out in the woods at all for that matter. Yet Jerry's conscience told him he must warn Clifford about those two men. After all, it was only thanks to Clifford that he had acquired Brill. So he decided to ring the hospital and tell Clifford he'd got news for him — on condition he agreed not to contact any of the authorities about what he'd heard from Artie.

The telephone rang at Ripley Manor. Monica answered. 'Yes Nigel? What's the latest?'

'Well um ... you remember my telling you about Sarah and the little French dog.'

'That's something I could not easily forget.'

'She's picked it up — dead.'

'Has she indeed? Well I trust you've given it a very deep grave.'

'I haven't got round to that yet, I was about to cremate it.'

'Where's the body now?'

'When Sarah brought it back she was very upset, as you may imagine, and she asked me to dispose of it. I put it on top of our garden bonfire, which I didn't light right away as it was just when I'd heard Zebedee was still wandering around out there and I went looking for him again.'

'Well, the sooner you destroy all evidence of Coco the better. He has to be the prime suspect.'

'I intend to do just that.'

'Is Sarah with you now?'

'No — gone shopping.'

X

Lying in the white cocoon of his hospital bed, Clifford had received the news of the Council's emergency plans with some relief. Not only, he reckoned, would the good Puffin be safe, but no foreseeable harm would come to the other dogs either, and with any luck he'd be absolved of all responsibility for them. The rabies scare had at least provided that safeguard.

But Jerry Fuller's telephone call, put through just now, had filled him with great consternation and alarm. Although he knew nothing of the reputation of Hood or Candy Sewell's father they certainly sounded like a couple of hard and determined characters. Indeed, a rather gruesome duo. At first he thought that there was little action he, personally, could take to save the threatened dogs, particularly since he'd promised young Jerry he would say nothing to the police about the two men's intentions.

Meanwhile, it was imperative that Puffin be saved. And the only person he could think of who might be able to help him in this was old Monica. But to keep faith with Jerry Fuller he'd have to swear her to secrecy. The matron had moved him to a private ward, which he had to himself, and that was helpful.

In his enforced idleness, he made plans for the future.

I'm going to start walking towards the Downs and on to Beachy Head with Puffin as soon as I get out of this place and the dog problem is sorted out. But, Monica, home again would certainly blame me (not without good reason) for infesting the cabin with all those mutts. They'd be running around wild now, probably sniffing at the sinister Lupa, possibly all rabid. Oh, Lord! — supposing Puffin was bitten?

Perhaps the good Mrs Bowes-Onslow would take the view that all the work I've put into repairing and improving the cabin and its grounds would compensate for my irresponsibility in taking in those dogs? Pity I didn't finish the window sills, and . . . oh yes, the door of the outside loo. I've put off repairing that for much too long. Every time it rains the floor and walls of that hovel get more soaked and rotten. I've got to put it right before I leave for home. But all such thoughts were subordinate to his concern for Puffin. *How I'll blame and curse myself if anything happens to that little terrier! I must get out of here, this place is suffocating, and there is so much to do . . .*

Within ten minutes of his talk with Jerry he contacted Monica, who was sympathetic and most understanding about his problem regarding the dogs. And she shared his anxiety about Puffin. She tried to reassure him that there was only a remote possibility of the men with guns finding the dogs. Besides, it was dark now there was nothing she could do until dawn. But he must rest assured, she told him, that she would act resolutely as soon as it was light. He thanked her for her offer to visit him, but added that it would not be necessary because 'I'll be out of this place in no time'

. . . *Very sound and reliable woman thought Clifford,* replacing the receiver, pulling up the sheets and lying back on his pillows with a sigh of satisfaction and relief. *I feel fit as a fiddle,* he told himself. He was bored stiff with this sanitised ward. He listened in to himself, listened to his heartbeat. *There's nothing wrong with me, surely?* They had not drawn his curtains yet. He gazed out at the cloudless night with the moon high up in the starlit sky. *This would be a good time to find little Puffin. He'd come straight away to my call.* The sister entered to take his temperature.

'I'm perfectly well now, sister,' he smiled when she removed the thermometer. 'With all due respect to your hospitality I'd like to leave.'

'Ooh no, you can't do that Mr Clifford, the doctor wants to keep you in for a few days yet.'

Clifford gave a dismal sigh. 'A few days more, that's not necessary you know . . . By the way how's that little girl with the rabies bite?'

'She's going to be all right,' said the sister, puffing up his pillows, 'but she's not really over the trauma of it yet.'

'Well I'm over my trauma and I want to leave.'

'Now you just lie there and relax.'

Left alone again, Clifford drummed the blankets with his finger tips and thought hard, too hard for his own good. He was a man of powerful imagination and, in his present mood, a prey to erratically vivid and depressing images. He envisaged Monica failing to reach Puffin in time, saw Puffin being shot or battered to death with clubs. As such mental visions became stronger, so Clifford grew more agitated. Could he not let himself out of this soul-destroying place? They'd still got this absurd cardiac motor thing attached to him. Well, it could easily be switched off and unplugged. He listened to the weather forecast. It was not good.

Rabies or no rabies, to Monica the thought of men setting out at dawn with guns to shoot dogs that had been in the care of a man who was now lying in a hospital bed, was anathema. It would be sacrilege. *I have to go out and stop them, or at least make the effort. So one of them was a sheep farmer, a tenant of Edwin Harrington's. Well, well . . . Hood, yes that name was familiar. And Sewell was the father of the child who was bitten. Well, he had good reason for taking the law into his own hands . . .* She pondered as to why Mr Clifford's young informant had sworn him to secrecy regarding the authorities, and concluded that he feared having the dog, which he had just retrieved, confiscated. Not relishing the prospect of setting off in the early dawn by herself, she decided to enrol Nigel, the scene of action being his father's land. As she was thinking these thoughts the telephone rang. It was Nigel.

'I thought I'd just let you know, Monica, that the police have been on to me about Zebedee. Apparently, your Mr Clifford had him and gave a pretty good description including the little white tip to his tail, which is pretty rare for a black labrador . . .'

'Since the rabies outbreak,' replied Monica tartly, 'I'm much more concerned about the little brute that you and Sarah brought back from France. Have you burnt it yet?'

'I was coming to the question of Coco. This is a much bigger worry. Within an hour of Sarah returning with the dead body and me laying it on the bonfire just before dark, when we were both out, the Tillston dog warden turned up and asked the chap who works in the garden part-time whether he'd seen any strays around there. The gardener said no, but that there was a dead one on top of the rubbish that was due to be burned. Then the warden put Coco's corpse in a plastic sack and took it away with him.'

'Nigel, if I was in your shoes I'd be very anxious indeed about this.'

'I am.'

'They'll do tests, they'll prove rabid. Your beastly little

Coco answers the description given by the girl who was bitten. You and Sarah could do a long stretch in gaol.'

'I know.'

'Except for one thing, which is that my Sarah has never failed to wriggle out of any trouble she's been in. She's succeeded all her life. However, nothing can be done about all that for the time being. Your immediate problem is Zebedee.'

'Oh I'm not worried about him now. The authorities are putting down anti-rabies vaccine bait and he'll soon be rounded up.'

'Well, I hate to burden you with even more distress than you've got already, but another sinister factor has crept in which I'll tell you about if you promise to keep it to yourself.'

'I promise.'

'I have it on very good authority that a party of men are going out with guns first thing in the morning. They think the authorities are pussyfooting over this affair. Their leader is a tenant of your father's who had his sheep savaged. Bob Hood... You know him?... right. He reckons the strays are still packed together, and he knows exactly where they're lying up. Another member of the party is the father of the girl who was bitten. Their blood's up, these men...'

'Good God — Zebedee!'

'Well yes, but as for me I'm more concerned about the little terrier I gave Mr Clifford — Puffin, who's worth his weight in gold. Nigel, I'm thinking of setting off from here half an hour before first light to try and find him. How about joining me? You never know, you might pick up Zebedee.'

'Yes — yes certainly.'

'Good, you come up here at six-thirty then. You'd better not tell Sarah what you're doing. Or anyone else for that matter.'

'Certainly not.'

Turning from the telephone Monica was confronted by her brother.

'I couldn't help overhearing the last part of your talk,' said the vicar. 'So you're going out in the early morning looking for dogs. Well, I'm not letting you do that without me.'

His sister gave an exasperated sigh. 'No, no, Richard, there's no need for you to bother yourself. As you heard, Nigel will be with me.'

'Well, I'll be there too. I insist.'

'Heavens above!' exclaimed Monica. 'As though I haven't got enough to put up with. Oh, all right...'

'I know you'll appreciate my presence when the time comes.'

'It's a kind thought, Richard, but mind you get warm and waterproof, there's a storm brewing up. We'd better have an early bed.'

XI

The nurse, going on her rounds at midnight and seeing Clifford wide awake, hands behind his head and staring at the ceiling, offered him a sedative. He wouldn't take one. He wanted, above all, to remain awake. He was restless, full of dread. He put his hand over his heart, and felt and listened carefully. It was still even and regular. There had been no hint of the chest pains since that attack in the woods.

By about four o'clock in the morning he'd made his decision to leave the hospital and go looking for Puffin. He switched off and unplugged the cardiac motor they'd applied, then got up and opened his locker. He dressed quickly and silently, and gathered up his painting things. He crept silently past the night nurse, nodding with fatigue, and flitted downstairs past the porter, also half asleep. He pushed open the doors and, with great relief, breathed in the fresh brisk air of November. He was free, his own master again. Within half an hour, with the help of the moon, and walking routes already familiar to him, he was back in the cabin. There, he lit his primus and made himself some coffee and a couple of sandwiches. How refreshing it was to have put that claustrophobic hospital behind him!

Then, as the first fingers of light stole through the

branches of the Ripley woods he started his search for Puffin, gallant little brown-and-white Puffin whom he had missed so much these last couple of days. Some premonition drew him directly towards Snakey's grave. He stopped for two or three minutes there with a lump in his throat. The sky had been clouding over and now it began to rain, a heavy penetrating rain against which he was by no means adequately dressed.

'The woods are not too thick this side of the Avonlea stream,' whispered Bob Hood while he and his sons and Sewell approached the west side of Pheasant Copse as dawn was breaking. 'Dogs are almost certainly lying up straight ahead here. So we'll spread out on a 150-yard front, forty yards apart, Ted and me in the middle, you two lads on the flanks, right?... When we reach the stream we'll close up on the bridge, then fan out again the far side, right?... Bloody hell, this rain'll affect our line of vision. On the other hand it'll also encourage the dogs to sit tight. OK, boys, let's get separated. The byword is stealth, go slow, go quiet, keep your eyes skinned...'

And so the four guns started their advance, the crackle of their waxed clothing and the shuffle of their feet on the leafmould muted by the patter of rain through the branches. After about ten minutes Sewell came across the bodies of Regal and Seagull. He called hoarsely to Hood, who signalled to his sons to halt and went over and examined the wet tricolour bodies closely. 'M'm rabies victims, I shouldn't wonder,' he said. 'Well, seeing these mutts have been moving around in a pack chances are the others won't be far away. Don't shoot, Ted, unless you're sure of killing. We'd better take it a bit slower now...'

Hood signalled for the drive to be resumed. They advanced very gingerly for a minute or two. Then a shot rang out. Hood ran over towards Sewell. 'What were you brassin' off at then?' he asked.

'Big grey devil out there!' Sewell pointed ahead half left.'

'Well you've missed it, haven't you!'

'Difficult to see in the rain, Bob.'

'Well, I said don't shoot till you were close didn't I. Now you've likely panicked them...'

Half an hour earlier the Reverend Richard Illingworth, wrapped in several thick cardigans as he appeared downstairs at Ripley, looked heavier than ever.

'I must say, it's a great surprise to find you so keen on joining our jaunt,' said his sister. 'Since when were you so keen on dogs? You soon got tired of Gannet if I remember rightly?'

'Have no fear, Monica, I shan't be helping you to find the wretched little terrier. It's your own welfare I'm interested in.'

Nigel Harrington arrived a minute later. 'There's been another drama up in our woods,' he said.

'Oh, what's that?' Monica handed him and her brother cups of tea.

'Some young man pushed dad into a ditch yesterday.'

'I suppose your father was being officious as usual,' Monica said with a caustic laugh.

'Probably.'

'How's Sarah?'

'Sound asleep and with orders to stay in all morning, which is just as well seeing it's clouding over black as hell just now.'

Monica looked at her watch. 'Well, if my information's right those men'll be starting out in a minute. We'd better get moving. Which route do we take?'

'Up to your footpath,' said Nigel, 'then right-handed down to the Avonlea footbridge and up towards the Temple. That's close to where I last saw Zebedee and it's where this Hood man said he reckoned they were. As we've got no moon now, I'll lead the way with a torch till it's light. When we've crossed the bridge, I suggest we separate a bit.'

Monica agreed and the three of them set off. Very soon they were walking under a driving rain. Illingworth, holding his umbrella aloft and skipping between the puddles in a vain attempt to keep his ankles dry, declared loudly how much he wished he'd worn gumboots like the other two. Monica snapped back at him, telling him to keep his voice to a whisper.

As they approached the footbridge the three of them were alerted by the shot that Sewell fired. Leaving Illingworth looking flustered, Monica and Nigel made their way onto the bridge and paused, glancing to right and left. Nigel whispered urgently: 'Phew, d'you see that Monica?'

'Where?'

'Up there among the trees, between you and me — looks like an alsatian.'

Lupa, the wolf-like cur, the *femme formidable* phantom of the forests, wild-eyed, rain-soaked and bedraggled but unscathed by Sewell's pellets, came in view of Monica. The bitch snarled, hackles up. She hesitated, careered down the bank, splashed into the swirling water and was up the other side in a flash, shaking her coarse grey-brown coat, then cantering on. 'Some alsatian!' Monica called 'Looks more like the Hound of the Baskervilles!'

Close behind Lupa another dog appeared, this time a

black labrador. Monica nudged Nigel. 'Here, Nigel, we could be in luck, I think we've got your Zebedee!' As the young gun dog stood there watching Monica, Nigel ran across and buckled a collar and lead on him; and Zebedee, looking starved and exhausted under his sodden coat, wagged his tail wearily. Nigel turned to Monica. 'Well, I'll leave you and Richard now if that's alright. The sooner I get him safely home the better. I'll return to the cottage via the side of the stream. I ought to avoid them that way.'

'Yes, and I shouldn't waste any time about it,' agreed Monica. 'Come up to Ripley after you've got him home and when this business is over, will you Nigel?'

'I'll do that.'

When Nigel left, Illingworth caught up with his sister and they crossed the footbridge together. A minute later Ilingworth's precise voice was saying 'there's someone running up there, look!'

'Yes, so there is, come on Richard!' And Monica led the way from the bridge, between the trees up the hillside towards the Temple, with Illingworth panting and groaning loudly.

Wanting to avoid human contact, Clifford had crossed the brook by a ford he'd previously discovered, a couple of hundred yards below the footbridge. In his thin clothing he was shuddering like a jelly. His teeth chattered, and, while he climbed the slope a severe feeling of sickness and malaise came over him. But as he neared the Temple his heart gave a leap as he saw Puffin standing straight and very still, gazing in the opposite direction. The terrier was on the precise spot where Clifford's painting stool had been three days before. The moment Clifford spotted Puffin through the heavy curtain of rain, he broke into the fastest pace his energies could muster. A terrible dazzle came across his eyes, he felt very sick and there was a burning pain in his chest.

As he closed on Puffin two men emerged between the trees and, to his horror, he saw one of them raise his gun to his shoulder in a direct line at Puffin. 'Hold it! Don't shoot!' he yelled, raising his hands above his head while he strode on, despite the agony of his illness. Hearing the familiar voice Puffin turned, flicked his tail vigorously and ran a few paces in the direction of that voice. 'Don't fire!' Clifford shouted. But in the very moment he made that second anguished entreaty, a shot exploded. He collapsed, clutching his ribs, and lay face downwards on the ground.

Clifford's body spread contorted and prostrate on the very spot where, so recently and in apparently safe health, he had sat painting the Temple. Now the colour had drained from his face, his mouth was half open and his eyes were closed. Locks of his grey hair lay matted against his temples. Puffin, who had moved instantly at the sound of his voice, was now hunched on his shoulders, shivering against the biting rain. And with his head raised, he howled miserably. His ears, moments before, had been pricked to show their bent triangles, tawny and silky, above brown eyes glittering with delighted surprise to see Jack Clifford. They now lay back against his neck in utter dejection. Puffin knew Clifford was dead from the instant the last breath left his body.

Monica and her brother, having paced the final yards of the wooded slope puffing and blowing, reached the scene within thirty seconds of Clifford's collapse.

Ejecting the spent cartridge, Sewell strode towards Clifford. Hood was soon beside him. By the time the two men reached him Monica was already feeling Clifford's pulse, while Puffin still clung to his shoulders, shivering and whining.

'I fear the worst,' said Illingworth. 'I fear he has passed over.'

Monica gave Sewell a look of withering scorn. 'You killed him!' she rasped.

Sewell's blubbery face gazed back in horror, raindrops coursing down his cheeks like tears. 'I was shooting at the dog. Blighter moved as I squeezed the trigger.'

'Maybe,' said Monica, 'but as you see, you gave the man a heart attack from which he didn't recover.' She turned to Sewell's partner. 'You're Mr Hood, I think? You farm across the way?'

'That's right, I know you, too.'

'I'm surprised to find you involved in this.'

'Surprise or no surprise, Mrs Bowes-Onslow, the dogs hereabouts have been worrying my sheep, and as soon as you clear off home I'll be destroying this little dog.' Hood jerked his 12-bore towards Puffin.

'You'll do no such thing!' shouted Monica in high dudgeon. With a quick flourish she stooped to grab Puffin and held him tight against her waterproof jacket. Hood's sons had now closed in and she was addressing all four men. 'Anyhow, you should have more on your mind than killing dogs.' She nodded sadly at Clifford. 'This man was my tenant and I hold you responsible for his death. You're not to touch him. I'm going straight home now to ring the police.'

Hood had not yet admitted defeat. 'But this isn't your land, Mrs Bowes-Onslow, 'you've got no business of accusing us of anything on someone else's land.'

Puffin strained to return to Clifford and Monica used

all her strength to hold him. She looked down the slope towards Avonlea brook, across which her own estate began less than 200 yards away before facing Hood again. 'You've got no business up here either,' she reminded him, 'in view of the Council embargo. Anyhow, my land or no, I suggest you go and report yourselves to the police. Tell them about the tragedy you've caused and how you did it. I shall be getting them up here.'

'Well I'm not sure about that,' said Hood, 'when dogs go savaging shcep...'

'As a fellow farmer I have some sympathy with that,' Monica replied, 'but it doesn't alter my advice to you. If you leave directly and report to the police, my brother here and I might put in a mitigating plea for you.'

Hood's expression was one of surrender. He turned to each of his sons, then to Sewell. He jerked his head. 'Alright, come on then!'

And Monica and her brother, with sighs of relief, watched them move past the Temple and out of sight. 'You can leave Mr Clifford in my care,' Illingworth told her.

'Thank you.'

'I shall be praying for the soul of this poor misguided man. I shall stay till the police come.'

'You do that, Richard, while I take Puffin home with me.'

'Oh that wretched little terrier, the cause of all the trouble. I sometimes think the Almighty sent pets especially to test mankind's sense of reason.'

And so Monica left her brother to his ministrations. All the way to the house Puffin was struggling, looking back towards the place where his master had fallen. As soon as Monica was indoors she described the morning's drama to Mrs Harris. 'Extraordinary what a charmed life this little dog has had. Missed being shot by Jarrow by inches and now, a few days later, the same thing happens on exactly the same spot. Puffin must have been born under a very lucky star.'

'He's not as other dogs are is Puffin,' said Mrs Harris.

XII

Sarah scarcely glanced at Zebedee when Nigel, his waterproofs dripping, returned to the cottage with the labrador. 'Oh, thank God you're back!' she said, tearfully. Coco's body's gone, d'you know what's happened to him?'

Nigel assumed that Coco had by now passed through a laboratory and been certified a rabies victim and that the little French dog would have been found posthumously guilty of biting the girl on the swing. But, although he was fairly convinced of those procedures, he had no intention of telling Sarah about the removal of Coco's body by the Tillston dog warden or his speculation as to the sequel. 'Coco's corpse gone? How awful,' he said, 'must've been taken by a fox. But don't let's worry about that now, darling. . . '

'By a fox? Oh, poor little thing.'

Nigel changed the subject. 'Well isn't it wonderful I've got Zebedee back.'

'Zebedee, yes,' she said, looking abstractedly at the black labrador. 'But he's too wet and muddy to be in here. Leave him in the back porch please, Nige.'

'All right. Will you look after him while I pay your mother a visit?'

Sarah looked at her husband with disdainful surprise.

'What are you going to see her for?'

'Well — she wants to talk to me about that man she lent the cabin to.'

'Alright, I'll watch Zebedee, darling. But oh! — I can't get over poor little Coco being taken by a fox. I wanted to cremate him if and when this beastly rain ever stopped, and then give his ashes a Christian burial...'

After getting his absentee labrador a large warm meal, Nigel rubbed him dry with an old bathroom towel and settled him in a deep bed of newspaper. He then drove to Monica's house. It was midday by the time he got to Ripley.

'What news of your Mr Clifford?' he asked as Monica led him through to the library. Illingworth was standing at the french windows frowning at the rain. He turned briefly and nodded at Nigel. Puffin, with a place by the fire and still dismally, if quietly, moaning, had put a couple of yards between himself and the three spaniel bitches who were also lying on the hearth rug.

'Mr Clifford died at the Temple just after you left us,' Monica replied. 'Heart attack. He was such a nice man, self-absorbed and eccentric but a very good sort really. The police are up there. I suppose they'll be wanting to question me about him before the day's out.'

'Poor man. It was coming sooner rather than later.'

'He saved Puffin's life...'

'How was that?'

'Well, the moment one of those men took a shot at Puffin, the terrier saw Mr Clifford and dashed towards him. So the shot missed by inches.'

'Any other news?'

'A couple of beagles have been picked up, dead. A vet was called out. He reckoned they were rabies cases, so I hear. You were lucky to save Zebedee... I keep wondering what's become of that huge wild-looking alsatian thing that crossed the Avonlea brook when we were down there.'

'It seemed familiar somehow. I'm sure I've come across it before, but I can't place it. Perhaps that was rabid too.'

'It looked crazy, but fit enough, to me... When the rain's stopped, which it seems to be doing, I'll take a walk to the cabin and see what's been going on there. Will you join me?'

'Certainly.'

Illingworth turned from the windows. 'Would you like me to come, too, Monica? I could arrange the disposal of Mr Clifford's effects.'

'No thank you, Richard. Nigel and I will manage. I suggest you go along now and see what's being done about the funeral. You know the man's family situation.'

'Yes, I do — I will, good idea,' Illingworth agreed.

Monica waited till the door was closed, then reclined in the corner of a sofa and beckoned Puffin onto her knee. 'I didn't want to raise the subject while Richard was with us,' she said to Nigel, 'but what's Sarah up to?'

'At home mourning the loss of her little dog.'

'Tell me a bit more about that dog will you.'

Nigel related the entire Coco saga so far as he knew it. 'So they're sure to have carried out a post-mortem on the wretched thing and he's bound to be found guilty of biting the girl on the swing...'

'And introducing rabies to the United Kingdom,' added Monica.

'Yes, everything points to Coco. Doubtless he's now been through some laboratory and the police'll be on to us at any moment. Naturally, I will accept full responsibility.'

'It sounds to me — apart from your weakness in the matter — as though Sarah's entirely to blame.'

'Frankly, I don't think she's up to a court appearance

and all that, it'd be much better if I own up and handle everything. I shall no doubt receive a very hefty fine.'

'You could just as easily go to prison. The authorities take a very serious view of the illegal importation of animals.'

Monica stroked Puffin's back thoughtfully and gave a deep sigh. 'Oh, Sarah, Sarah, dear pretty Sarah.' She repeated the words more to herself than to her son-in-law. 'That child's spent her life getting away with murder. Her father spoilt her, gave her the impression she could do no wrong, laughed at her peccadilloes, hated rebuking her. Now *you*...'

'I'm not having her facing a police interrogation, a conviction, and...'

'That's just what her father would have said. She's always been brilliant at the 'poor little me' game, making people feel sorry for her. Ah well... Look, it's stopped raining, are you ready to go to the cabin?'

'Right.'

'I can't risk taking the spaniels, but I don't think little Puffin could possibly cause any harm. Come along Puffin! ... Oh blast there's the telephone. You take it, will you, Nigel.'

Nigel rejoined a somewhat impatient Monica at her front door five minutes later. 'Sorry to keep you waiting,' he said. 'That was Sarah. The police were round at the cottage with the dog warden. They asked her to confirm Coco was hers. They said he'd been proved rabid and that his description tallied exactly with that given by the child who was bitten.'

'So — what was Sarah's reaction?'

'She admitted Coco belonged to us, but said that he was a wedding present 'from a friend in Hampshire' and that he must have been bitten by a rabid fox.'

'That's typical of her,' said Monica, starting off across

the garden in the direction of the cabin. 'She's a deceitful little so-and-so. You may let her get away with it, Nigel, but I'm damned if I will. I'm going to tell them the truth. I don't mind how much trouble I get you both into. The authorities need to establish how rabies got here in the first place. If Sarah's cock-and-bull story is accepted they'll have nothing to work on.'

'Alright, you win, Monica, but as I say I'll take all the blame for it, if you don't mind.'

Having reached this decision, Nigel walked with his mother-in-law, in mutual silence, to the cabin.

'It's really marvellous what poor unfortunate Mr Clifford achieved,' Monica remarked. 'Floorboards repaired, new window frames, roof patched up, door mended — and look, Nigel, he's completely renewed the balustrade round the verandah. The whole place is almost as I first knew it.'

'He certainly didn't owe you any rent.'

'And see how he tidied up round the pond, he really was a marvel.'

'Here, take a look at this!' Nigel was thumbing through the cartridge papers of Clifford's latest watercolour sketchbook. 'These are really clever . . .'

Monica came round to his side. 'Oh, that's the Temple! It looks as though he was interrupted in the middle of it.'

'And here's a masterly one of a couple of beagles.'

'Yes we know about those, don't we. Oh, this whole business is so tragic and terrible.'

Nigel's face brightened at the next page. 'And there's Zebedee, a brilliant one of Zeb. I'd like to have that . . . So Clifford really was responsible for bringing the pack together.'

Monica turned the next two pages. 'Several of Puffin needless to say . . . he really loved Puffin . . . and here, this is rather a sweet one.' Monica pointed to Clifford's sketch of Coco.

'Ah — the villain of the piece.'

'We'd better turn over a new leaf,' said Monica doing so. I'm going to ask his next-of-kin if we can hang onto these pages, they're exquisite... Look, Puffin wants to be let out.'

'Have you any idea who the next of kin'd be?' asked Nigel opening the cabin doors for Puffin.

'Well, he mentioned grown-up young when I originally spoke to him. I imagine they'll be traced soon enough.'

'They could hardly refuse you these pictures seeing they're all of dogs and scenes around here.'

'He showed me an earlier book of pencil sketches he'd made on his hike. They'd keep those, of course... Oh listen to Puffin raising hell. What's he yapping about, I wonder?' Monica stepped outside and glanced round the back of the building. 'There — he's found something to interest him in the old loo.'

'Probably a rolled-up hedgehog. Nothing of any size could fit in there. I've known dogs bark all day at a hedgehog when they're left to it... That loo's something Mr Clifford didn't get round to mending,' said Nigel, taking note of the unhinged door.

'Never mind, he's made a wonderful job of everything else. A talented man, kind, lonely, strange. He hiked here — all the way from Beachy Head, if you please! And no chicken, either. The afternoon he knocked on my door he'd just had his dog, a lurcher, poisoned. It wasn't far from the spot where he himself was to die. He'd lost his wife only a couple of months before that. I think he'd looked on that lurcher as the last close living link with her. They were both mad about the dog, so he told me. I'm not certain he had a great deal to live for... It seems he had a lot of very peculiar prejudices. Richard — who's so good with people, usually, you know — couldn't get through to him at all . . .' Monica looked at her watch. 'It's time for a very late lunch, Nigel. Let's go . . . Come on, Puffin!'

But Puffin remained at the entrance to the cedarwood privy. His yapping was now reduced to whimpering. He seemed transfixed, bewitched.

'Oh well, if he finds a hedgehog more interesting than us who can blame him?' quipped Nigel, following through the rhododendron exit of the cabin compound. 'Tell me, Monica, are you going to keep Puffin at Ripley now?'

'No, I'm not, I've decided to send him away.'

'Oh, why's that?'

'Well the Puffin saga's full of traumas. His dam came to me as a stray and gave birth to her litter soon afterwards. Then the dam — Gannet was her name, I called her Foxy — was claimed by a young woman living on the other side of Guildford, a Mrs Peterson. Puffin got landed with some rather unsatisfactory local people who couldn't cope with him, so I took him back. But he doesn't get on at all well with the spaniels, you know, they've always bullied him . . . He was obviously happy with Mr Clifford. He must miss him terribly . . .'

'So what'll you do with him?'

'I'm going to offer him to Mrs Peterson.'

'So he'll be back with his dam. He couldn't ask for more than that.'

'I'm going to telephone Rose Peterson this evening.'

Monica and her son-in-law were half-way back to the house when Nigel said 'that big wild German Shepherd type that careered over the brook this morning when we were standing on the bridge, I've just remembered . . .'

'Yes?'

'It was the one facing Coco, I'm sure of it, the morning after we brought him back, and Coco followed it into the woods. It was the last we saw of him.'

'Well that's amazing, it's probably been living on its wits for months.'

'It *was* an eerie brute wasn't it.'

'Yes, let's forget about dogs for a bit, they can be a load of trouble...'

At first it was an uncertain canine odour rising from the decayed cedarwood latrine hut that had caught Puffin's attention. Then very cautiously, nose twitching, hackles up, he had edged forward stealthily to peer inside. And there — curled up like a fox, her nose buried in her tail, wrinkling her lip to show Puffin her yellow teeth and giving a very low hostile growl — was Lupa.

Like those nymphs of Homer's legends, the sirens, whose songs lured sailors to destruction, Lupa's interest in males appeared to lie largely in the power she could exercise over them. Her pleasure seemed to be in domination, in her mastery over male dogs. Her howling drew them to her from far away and her fragrance at close quarters, together with the bewitching sight of her in season, kept them in thrall. It was not, however, a joyous thrall, but more the sort that enslaves humans to a habit, like drugs.

It was dangerous for male dogs to be drawn into Lupa's web. She had been the source of most of the troubles of those last few days of Puffin's life at Ripley. For Coco, the rabies carrier, only strayed because of Lupa. If Regal and Seagull had not encountered Lupa they would have been saved the bites of the rabid Coco; they would almost certainly have been retrieved and returned to the laboratory in which they had led quite contented lives. And Candy Sewell would not have suffered if the dogs had not strayed to be with Lupa and wandered up to the Tillston playground. Zebedee enjoyed Lupa's favours, but that was a fleeting passion. From the moment he disappeared in Rockingham copse on the afternoon of the pheasant shoot to the moment he was reunited with Nigel, Zebedee was mostly uneasy and afraid.

Brill, after being liberated from his life of hell with the Sewells and escaping death in the vet's surgery, enjoyed two blissful weeks in Clifford's company. From Lupa, however, he had nothing but trouble, including a severe mauling. He was extremely fortunate to be retrieved by Jerry Fuller and saved from the possibility of being shot.

Lupa, worldly-wise bitch, had always been a survivor. Unlike the genuine domestic dog which loves the hand that feeds it and puts its faith and trust in man, Lupa both hated and feared human beings. And like many truly wild animals, she had learned how to avoid them and their traps and guns and poisons. She, unlike her male worshippers, was uncannily aware of the meaning of that gunshot sounding from the east in the early hours of the morning.

It was as well for her that Clifford never got around to mending and closing the door of the cedarwood privy hut behind the summer-house. Lupa may have had it in mind as a bolt-hole before she raced away from the gunfire in that direction. She was able to conceal herself almost completely among some sacks behind the seat. The council people made a fairly thorough search of the woods, but none thought of looking in there. Nor should they have done because, as Nigel Harrington had remarked, it was an unlikely place to find an animal of any significant size. 'Probably a hedgehog,' he had said when he saw Puffin taking an interest. Lupa was unique in more ways than simply her strange demeanour, her physical power, strength of character and sexual attraction.

That night when Monica let the dogs out for a run, a distant howling drew Puffin again. Three days before, he had bravely denied Lupa that squirrel he caught and even had her slinking away from it. Now, instead of trotting with the jaunty air that Clifford had so much admired, he appeared more like a naughty schoolboy sent for by the headteacher. Although his eyes were bright and eager, his ears and tail were carried low. His excited anticipation seemed to be mixed with a weird dread.

When Puffin arrived at the cabin Lupa remained silent, simply curling her tongue round her grey muzzle with a satisfied lick and staring back at them, triumph glinting in her yellow eyes. She appeared to take little notice when he lay watching her through the night, staring as a lizard might stare, transfixed, at the snake which intends to eat it up. The strange phenomenon was that she was no longer on heat and yet the power remained. Puffin returned to the house just as Monica was letting out the spaniels again. And she noticed how strangely subdued he seemed to be.

When Rose Peterson arrived the following afternoon to collect him, his demeanour changed at once. She cast an altogether different spell on him, a sparkling, cheerful spell. Rose had a way with all animals. And Gannet was in her car. Puffin recognised his dam unhesitatingly and with delirious terrier joy. Since then, ensconsed in that happy Peterson environment, Puffin has been utterly contented, undisturbed by further dreams of Lupa. Jack Clifford, meanwhile, lies buried in a churchyard close to Beachy Head.

This being essentially Puffin's chronicle, it moves with him, in mid-November, away from Ripley to Rose

Peterson's home, Wealdendale Farm in Sussex. We therefore have no first-hand evidence of what happened to Nigel and Sarah Harrington. We can only quote the newspaper reports which said that for Nigel there was terrible retribution. Having come clean about Coco, he was tried, and received the heaviest penalty the British judiciary was allowed to award. At the time of writing, according to the *Gazette*, Candy Sewell's father is awaiting trial on charges of being in possession of, and firing, a shotgun without a licence and of causing grievous bodily harm.

As for Lupa, we can only conjecture whether she gave birth to puppies by Zebedee with whom she copulated at the very peak of her season. But we do know that her phantom noises have continued to be heard in the Leawood, Brinkworth and Ripley woods, and that one or two Tillston residents have caught glimpses of her around outlying dustbins during the night, reporting them with the same sort of emphatic conviction of people claiming to have seen the Loch Ness monster. Perhaps she is still there, living by her crafty wiles.

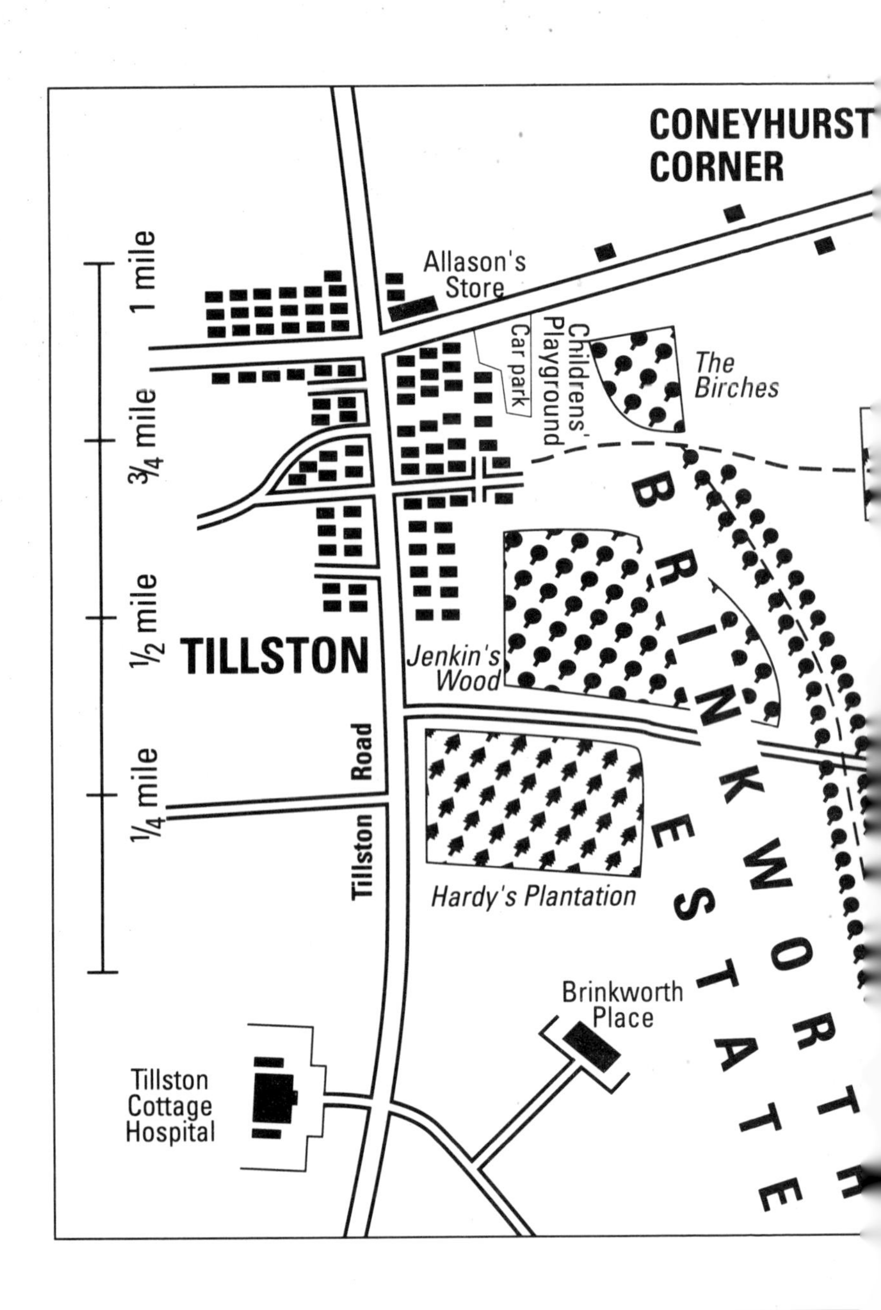
CONEYHURST CORNER
Allason's Store
Childrens' Playground
Car park
The Birches
BRINKWORTH ESTATE
TILLSTON
Jenkin's Wood
Tillston Road
Hardy's Plantation
Brinkworth Place
Tillston Cottage Hospital
1/4 mile
1/2 mile
3/4 mile
1 mile